Margaret Cathcart pushed through the crowded room...

...and stared at the lovely antique dollhouse.

"Where did you ever find such a beautiful thing?" she asked, turning toward its elderly owner.

But the owner was in no condition to reply. Dropping her wineglass, Marion Bundy clutched at her stomach, her mouth gaping mutely, her eyes pleading for help. And before Margaret could move, Marion had fallen to the floor, her body twisted with pain.

The others in the room froze in horror—except for one, who looked more puzzled than surprised.

Keeping you in suspense is our business

RAVEN HOUSE takes pride in having
its name added to the select
list of prestigious publishers
that have brought—in the
nearly one and one-half centuries
since the appearance of the
first detective story—the finest
examples of this exciting
literary form to millions of readers
around the world.

Edgar Allan Poe's
The Murders in the Rue Morgue
started it all in 1841.
We at RAVEN HOUSE are proud
to continue the tradition.

Raven House Mysteries

Let us keep you in suspense.

a Fragrant DEATH

Christina Blake

A RAVEN HOUSE MYSTERY FROM
WORLDWIDE
TORONTO · LONDON · NEW YORK

Debbie, Pam and Chris

Raven House edition published September 1981

Second printing September 1981

ISBN 0-373-63001-8

1

"NOTHING EXCITING ever happens in the country," whined the woman with the orange curls, as the train swayed through the brown and green countryside.

Anyone would have been quick to see that the two women sitting opposite the speaker in the train compartment were as different as night and day, and each reacted characteristically to the remark.

The tall slim one, elegantly clothed in a plum-colored traveling suit, with a spray of pink velvet roses nestled in her beautifully coiffed gray hair, kept her eyes downcast on the romantic novel she was reading, her patrician features betraying not a sign that she had even heard the remark, let alone that she might harbor any thoughts on the matter.

But the other woman, shorter and more sturdily built, could not contain an audible sigh of impatience. A tolerance of complainers was not one of Margaret Cathcart's strong points, and for the past hour, ever since the train had pulled out of Paddington station, this person with the flame-colored hair had been verbalizing aloud, to no one in particular, about her discontent with the journey.

Unlike her seat companion's fastidious attire,

Margaret's clothes were chosen for personal com-
fort and practicality, rather than for smartness.
At present, her large-boned frame was enveloped
in her usual attire: a belted beige mac, reinforced
stockings and sturdy brogues—in Margaret's
opinion, the only sensible things to wear in un-
predictable English weather. She did, however,
allow herself one flight of fashion, and that ex-
travagance lay in her choice of hats. And to
prove this point, she had a closet full of them.
Whether this excessiveness was a form of self-
expression, she never questioned; all she knew
was that she could never pass a millinery shop
without trying on several hats. . .and the more
outlandish the style, the more she liked it.
Which, as many of her friends had often said,
was rather handy if Margaret was lost in a crowd.
Just look for the most ridiculous hat, and there
she was under it!

And today, true to form, perched on mouse-
brown hair, was a bilious-green straw hat,
blocked into an exaggerated Robin Hood form
and sporting a foot-long quail feather that protruded at a forty-five degree angle from just
above the right ear. Completing the ensemble,
sitting beside Margaret's feet, was a brown
leather valise, with an umbrella tucked through
the handles. If dress was any indication of family
affiliation, one would never take these two
women sitting side by side to be sisters—which,
in fact, they were.

"You could live all your blessed life in the
country and never have any excitement," continued the talker, looking out the train window.
"Give me London any time!"

You could live all your life in London and never

have any excitement, thought Margaret wryly.

She followed the woman's gaze outside the window and had to admit that the pastoral scene of soft green pastures and lazy, grazing farm animals was a far cry from bustling London and certainly did create a deceptive air of placidness. But underneath it all, Margaret knew that the setting didn't make any difference; human nature was the same everywhere.

Despite her annoyance with the litany of complaints, Margaret's natural friendliness and curiosity got the better of her, and smiling across, she caught the woman's eye. "Are you going on holiday?" she asked, knowing full well she probably wasn't.

The woman returned a wary smile, unsure of herself; but trust overcame apprehension when she saw the sincerity in Margaret's eyes, and the smile widened. "Oh, no, dearie, I'm going to a place called Kingscombe—a little fishing village near Plymouth—to help out a cousin who's going on holiday."

"Kingscombe!" exclaimed Margaret. "Good heavens! My sister and I are going there, too! Have you been there before?"

The orange curls shook a firm negative response. "Never. If me cousin, Joyce Twickham—she runs the post office—wasn't so bent on going to a wedding...." She sighed, then went on, "She has no one else, you see, to help her out, so I said I'd manage the shop for a few days. Mind," she cautioned, "I wouldn't do it for everyone, but Joyce is sort of special. Our mums were sisters," she added as though that fact should explain everything.

"But we know Miss Twickham!" said Marga-

ret. "We're visiting a relative, too. Colonel Hawkins. He's opening up a toy museum."

"Oh?" said the woman indifferently. "I don't
have much to do with toys, not since me boys
have grown up." Then, to close the matter, she
glanced significantly at Margaret's wrist and
asked, "What time is it?"

Margaret looked at her black-strapped watch.
"Almost seven o'clock," she said. "They'll be
opening the dining car for breakfast any minute
now."

"Arh, that's not for me," said the woman,
reaching into a string shopping bag from which
she extracted a red plastic thermos and a wax-
paper-wrapped, somewhat misshapen sandwich.
"Can't abide the stuff they serve in public places
nowadays and have the nerve to call food."

Somewhat relieved that she and her sister
would not have to endure a volley of complaints
during breakfast, Margaret glanced over at Elizabeth, who, throughout the discourse had kept
her gaze steadfastly fixed on the book before
her. Now she rapidly placed her marker on the
page and snapped the covers shut, obviously only
too glad to be getting out. "Well, I think we'd
better, Margaret," she said rising. Then with a
gentle, "We'll see you later," to their train companion, she followed the already retreating back
of her sister out into the passageway, closing the
door behind her.

The breakfast choices were as unpalatable and
unimaginative as the usual train fare, and
Margaret, stirring cream into her coffee, while
Elizabeth spread marmalade on her toast, found
herself reflecting upon the orange-haired
woman's remark, "Nothing exciting ever hap-

pens in the country.'' As much as she disliked
such flat statements, she had to admit that Kingscombe had always been a quiet village. Tucked in
the hills of the Devon coast, it was touted as one
of the most picturesque villages in England, with
a fifteenth-century inn, several black and white
Tudor houses and two thatched-roof fourteenth-
century houses that were still in everyday use.
She'd visited the village so often it was like a
second home, and Charles Hawkins was more
like an older brother than a cousin twenty years
her senior.

A smile formed on her face as she thought of
some of the good times she'd had there. Yes, she
loved Kingscombe, with its narrow lanes, bor-
dered with green hedgerows and ivy-covered
stone walls that ran invitingly higgledy-piggledy
off the High Street with its small cluster of shops.
But no matter what one said, it really wasn't an
exciting village, even taking into account the un-
predictability of human nature. Margaret sipped
her coffee. Kingscombe was, in fact, thought
Margaret flatly, a rather sleepy place. And, she
supposed, it probably would remain that way.

In the days to come, she would realize how
very wrong that notion was, for even while Margaret Cathcart was musing about her destination,
Emily King, already an unsuspecting victim of
events, was lying in her bed upstairs at Rose Hill
Cottage on Viceroy Lane, Kingscombe, vividly
reliving a nightmare from which she'd just awakened.

2

SHE REMEMBERED she'd screamed. Someone had pushed her into a deep, vertical tunnel, and as her body tumbled head over heels, she could see the light at the top one second and then, as she turned, nothing but blackness.

Fear...fear of the unknown had been her prime emotion, but then, as her body had straightened itself out and she began to fall faster, sheer panic had set it. Frantically, she'd thrown out her arms, putting her hands against the walls of the tunnel in a vain attempt to slow her descent; but excruciating pain stabbed at her fingers as they made contact, and she quickly withdrew them, horrified to find them lacerated and bloody. Then, quite suddenly, a shrill, penetrating whistle had punctured her brain. Clamping her hands over her ears, she'd begun to scream.

Bong...bong...bong.... The grandfather clock on the hall landing had awakened her. She remembered that quite clearly. She had looked at her bedside clock, and the luminous numbers had indicated it was 3:00 A.M. But nothing that followed made sense. Even now, as she lay in bed, with the faint morning sunlight filtering into the room, both her mind and body balked at reviewing this illogical sequence; but with great concentration, Emily closed her eyes and forced herself to remember. . . .

She remembered she had lain there a few minutes, adjusting to the fact that she'd had a bad dream, and then she'd realized her throat was dry and she needed some water.

She'd thrown back the covers and picked up her robe from the foot of the bed. She'd gone out to the hall and down the stairs to the bathroom, where she'd drunk a glass of cold water. Then she'd made her way back to her room and glanced at the clock again—it had registered a little after three. She'd crawled back into bed. . . and then came the frightening part. She remembered that, as she was drifting off to sleep, the disquieting thought that her throat was still dry had persisted, and finally, in annoyance, she'd attempted to kick off the covers and get up. It was at this point that she experienced a shocking realization: although she clearly remembered going through the motions of getting a drink, she hadn't actually been out of bed! And then she discovered *she couldn't get out of bed!* Her body wouldn't respond to command! She remembered how panicky she'd become, how she'd concentrated, willed herself to sit up. . .but nothing had happened! Even now, this morning, thinking about it made her break out in a cold sweat.

With renewed determination, she kept her thoughts focused on what had happened next. There had been the sharp sound of a motorboat starting up in the bay, and shortly after that she'd heard water running. Where? Kitchen? Bathroom. . .? She recalled that she'd desperately tried to call out, but that no sound was forthcoming. She could hear everything going on

around her, but she couldn't move, couldn't
even make a sound!

She remembered lying there, helpless, sweat
pouring from her body, panic and confusion
within her. Finally, out of desperation, some corner of her mind told her body to force itself to
relax...to sleep...things would be better when
daylight came, and frantically, thankfully, she'd
grabbed at this small ray of hope. She vaguely
remembered the grandfather clock tolling a quar-
ter after the hour before she fell into a deep
slumber.

Emily's mind returned to the present, and she
opened her eyes. From her supine position, her
eyes moving from left to right, she methodically
assessed the large pieces of furniture in her bedroom: the mahogany armoire, the blue chair, the
draped vanity table, the rosewood bookcase.
Everything was intact. With some anxiety, she
lifted her right arm and looked at her hand. The
fingers moved perfectly. She smiled, relieved. It
really was morning, and she was wide awake,
and the knot of fear that had developed in her
stomach when she'd been reliving the nightmare
began to abate. It had really been a dream after
all. Everything was all right.

This time, throwing back the covers, she sat
up...then abruptly fell back, pressing both
hands to her head. Her first thought was that, if
she didn't know better, she had a king-sized
hangover... but how did one acquire that without drinking the night before? Suddenly, the
knot of fear returned. Hastily, in an effort to
quell it, she tried to rationalize. Maybe she was
coming down with the flu. She analyzed her
body. Her stomach wasn't queasy, her limbs

weren't sluggish, and she didn't even feel tired. No, boiled down, her symptom was simply a headache—true, a whopper of a one, but then, considering the night she'd had. . . .

For ten minutes she lay there, conscious only of the pounding in her head. Suddenly the clock on the landing boomed eight-thirty and she decided that if she was going to open up the Bell by ten, then she'd better get a move on. Gingerly, she once again made a tentative effort to raise her head. Surprisingly, it remained intact.

Very slowly, keeping her head as still as possible, Emily sat up and swung her legs over the side. Looking neither right nor left, she felt for her robe at the foot of the bed, found it and wrapped it around herself, while at the same time shoving her feet into fluffy white mules. Again, without turning her head, she opened the drawer in the lamp table and groped for the aspirin box. Flipping open the lid, she found only one aspirin, which she put in the pocket of her dressing gown. Then, gently massaging her temples, she slowly made her way out to the hall and down the stairs to the bathroom.

Twenty-five minutes passed before she returned to her room. She was still feeling far from one hundred percent, although a cold, needle-hard shower and the aspirin had subdued the acute pounding to a rhythmic dull throb. She could even move her head from side to side without increasing the pain. Opening the casement above the window seat, Emily drew in a few deep breaths of the clear salt air. "Therapeutic, the sea air," her mother had often said. Well, she certainly hoped her mother had been right and the therapy would start working on her headache.

The view from her bedroom window had never ceased to exhilarate her, but this morning that usual happy feeling didn't come. Emily moved back into the room and slowly and methodically began to dress. When she was satisfied with her appearance, she moved over to the window once again. Sitting on the window seat, she looked out.

Rose Hill cottage was built on a knoll, midway between the harbor and the village proper, offering a magnificent ocean view. She was happy to see that the previous night's storm had blown over and left a sky unmarred by cloud. The sun splayed diamonds on a calm cobalt sea, and the deep red cliffs, almost black in shadow, rose majestically from the sand beach to reach the blue sky. Here and there wisps of vapor could be seen rising from the downs as the sun burned off the early-morning mist. In the harbor, two white yachts, one flying the blue and yellow flag of Sweden and the other bearing the French standard, rode anchor amidst the smaller cruisers and sailboats, with their attendant dinghies bobbing gently on the rippling surface. The Lebanese freighter that had ridden out of the harbor with yesterday's high tide and sat crested on the horizon during the night, waiting to continue her journey today, had already disappeared from view. At the docks, she could discern small local fishing boats being emptied of the night's catch, and outside the harbor perimeter, still in the open sea, were three more with their haul. Their mackerel, flatfish and crabs were sold primarily in Kingscombe and surrounding villages. Fish not sold to the tradespeople were, by ancient custom hung on the "line"—a hauser rope located at the path leading down to the harbor. The fish, hanging at the mercy of the flies and weather, lasted but a short time, however, as there were always people waiting to take advantage of buying directly from the fisherman for considerably less than they'd pay in the shops.

The sea road, which ran along the top of the cliff, was hedged in by a row of gaily painted houses with tidy fenced yards and signs on the front gates denoting bed-and-breakfast accommodation. A souvenir shop, restaurant and a pub were tacked on at the end of the houses on the ocean side, and across from them were a few old shops, now refurbished and renewed, as well as a bingo hall and a laundromat. Aside from playing bingo, sitting on the beach, or sipping a pint at the bar, there were actually no holiday diversions for the tourist in Kingscombe. The little seaside houses were booked solid, however, because the rate was so much less than that in many of the neighboring towns that offered stage shows featuring television stars and a variety of bustling shops and fancy restaurants. If a Kingscombe tourist wanted to enjoy these amusements, all he had to do was take a fifteen-minute bus ride in either direction.

Overlooking the harbor was the fifteenth-century church, and the seventeenth-century vicarage. In deep contrast with the tangled, weed-choked cemetery on one side of the church, the vicarage garden was bursting in a kaleidoscope of hues, and while Emily was admiring the mass of color, she saw Miss Purdy, the vicar's sister, emerge from the church storage shed. Unmistakable in her broad-brimmed, gaily patterned Jamaican straw hat, she was dragging a sack, of what Emily guessed could only be fertilizer, over to one of the flower beds. Then she knelt, picked something up and started to dig.

The harbor area Emily saw from her window was the Kingscombe as the casual visitor saw it, and although there was a white signpost opposite the church with the words "Kingscombe 1/2 mi." and an arrow pointing toward a narrow paved road that ran inland, very few tourists took time to explore the village proper.

Ever mindful of her headache, Emily began to lightly brush her hair. Her panoramic eye focused on the distant Tudor chimneys of Harewood Hall, and despite her discomfort, a small smile formed on her lips as she thought about the party that evening.

Harewood Hall was the home of Colonel Charles Hawkins, whose family had been mostly army people for two hundred years and who had occupied the same impressive abode for almost that same number of years. The Hall, now with empty stables and coach house, was a half mile or so from the harbor, and set back from the road on twenty-two acres of parkland comprising an Italian-style sunken lily pond, a one-acre trout lake, a tennis court and winding walks through shrubs and trees. The Hall itself had overhanging gables, tall chimneys, white plaster walls, a roof of mellow brick tiles, and leaded glass windows. The scene of much activity lately was the old coach house, which would soon open its doors as the Victorian Toy Museum; the colonel's forebears had amassed a considerable collection of toys in the same manner as other families of like means collected miniature paintings, china or snuffboxes.

Although he was opening the museum partly for monetary reasons—maintaining the Hall was costly—he also had another motive, one that would have been sufficient even if he had not needed the money. He was bored. An active man all his life, on retirement he had found the large house too quiet for his temperament, and a time-consuming project seemed to be the answer to his problem. And so the idea of the Victorian Toy Museum was born. For months the colonel scoured the countryside to round out his collection. The big day, opening day, was only one week away, and tonight he was giving a dinner party for a select few to preview the museum's treasures.

Looking at the harbor, Emily had a fleeting thought of the motor she'd heard during the night. Had she really heard it? Or had it been part of the dream? The question made her head pound, and determinedly she forced it from her mind just as the clock struck the hour.

Quickly, but still careful not to jar her head, she made her bed. There was a gentle knock on the door, and Ruth Dawson, the daily help at Rose Hill, popped her head around. "Good morning, dear," she said with a smile. "Breakfast in five minutes. Just have to boil your egg."

Putting her hand to her forehead and sitting on the edge of the bed, Emily moaned, "Thank you, Mrs. Dawson, but no breakfast for me this morning. Just a cup of strong black coffee."

Registering motherly concern, Ruth Dawson went over to stand by the bed. "Oh? Not feeling up to par, dear? Anything I can get you?"

"No, thank you," said Emily. "I just have this beastly headache and an aspirin hasn't helped much. I'm hoping the coffee will."

"Right, dear." Exuding efficiency, Mrs. Dawson bustled toward the door. "It won't take but a minute and I'll make you some toast, too. A little food will do a world of good."

"No, nothing to eat, thanks. Just the coffee will be fine."

Undaunted by Emily's protest, Ruth Dawson went out into the hall with a firm, "Nonsense! Coffee and toast in five minutes!" Emily knew better than to argue, for Mrs. Dawson could be stubborn.

Childless and married to one of the local farm workers, Ruth Dawson had lived in Kingscombe all her life. She was a staunch, church-going woman, hard working and kind-hearted, but her personality had one blatant flaw. She had a penchant for gossip. Most of her acquaintances had long since made it a point never to tell her any thing they didn't want their neighbors to know. At present, however, Mrs. Dawson had forsaken any tidbits concerning her fellow villagers; the budding romance between Emily and John Trask, her employer's nephew, held her entire interest.

Five minutes later, downstairs and heading for the kitchen, Emily passed the door of her employer's bedroom. She smiled to herself when she thought of her first reaction to Sarah Loft.

Emily had been a nervous wreck after losing both parents in an auto accident, and her doctor had ordered three months' leave of absence from her job as an assistant curator in a large Toronto museum.

During a staff social gathering where she and several others had been discussing the pros and cons of where she should go and what she should do, one of the men—a research associate from mineralogy and a mere acquaintance of Emily's—had suggested a novel idea.

Only a few days ago, he said, he'd received a letter from a writer friend in England, a Sarah Loft, whose poor health had recently required her to move from London to the warmer climate of Devon. There she'd acquired a lovely two-bedroom renovated cottage and now was in need of a secretary-companion. He was sure the position wouldn't tax Emily too much—there was already a housekeeper—and she'd have a paid vacation to boot. He also assured her that Sarah was easy to get along with, and what the heck, if things didn't work out, she could always leave. What did she think? A telephone call would do the trick.

Emily asked for a couple of days to think it over, and as a result, three weeks to the day she had first heard Sarah's name, she met her hostess at London's Heathrow airport.

Emily's initial instinct when she saw Sarah was to turn around and buy a ticket for the next plane home. "Overwhelming" was the word that popped into her mind when Sarah introduced herself. A tall woman in her fifties, leaning on a sturdy, silver-topped ebony cane, she wore a floor-length dress in a red-and-pink cabbage-rose print, with long, full sleeves, and a high dog collar. (Emily was to learn later that Sarah's wardrobe contained only dresses, each of which completely covered her body). Her velvet choker was three inches wide, and upon her ample bosom rested several ropes of pearls—also Sarah's standard apparel. Her hands were resplendent with large rings, imbedded in the flesh of stubby fingers. Thick gray hair, parted in the center and elaborately waved, covered ears from which dangled one-inch pearl drops. She presented a rather terrifying figure, until one finally noticed the kind, chocolate-brown eyes, and the wide smiling mouth. She introduced the man standing next to her as her nephew, John Trask. His only similarity to his aunt was his height. Over six feet, with black wavy hair above a high forehead, a square; strong jaw and penetrating gray eyes, he smiled broadly and held out his hand in welcome.

The adjectives handsome, masculine, confident, along with half a dozen other flattering ones all filtered through Emily's mind as she returned his grasp. Here was a man a woman could not easily put out of her thoughts.

Emily took to Devon village life like a duck to a pond. Friendly, gossipy Mrs. Dawson had spent many hours over a period of six weeks enlightening her on the traits, talents and sins of the villagers.

And Sarah? She was kindness itself, and Emily couldn't have asked for a more thoughtful hostess. Since Sarah found it so laborious to move around, she had commissioned her nephew to be her guest's escort and guide for her stay. And John, who stayed at the Fox and Hound when in Kingscombe—Rose Hill, though pretty, was too small—fulfilled the role admirably, driving Emily to little out-of-the-way hamlets while at the same time making sure she saw the commercialized tourist spots. It soon became apparent to anyone within their realm that the two young people were taking more than a tourist-and-guide interest in each other. However, even though John came down from London on weekends and the odd weekday, Emily still found plenty of time on her hands. It hadn't taken long to catch up with Sarah's backlog of correspondence, and once that was done, her duties as secretary—primarily typing rough pieces of research for Sarah's book—took no more than two or three hours a day. Once that chore was completed, her time was pretty much her own; so while Sarah was closeted in her bedroom, writing, Emily took advantage of the time to explore Kingscombe.

Because of her background in antiquities, the place that held the most interest for her in the village was the antique shop, the Bell. A rather exclusive shop, it contained wonderful old bits and pieces, and quite often, to Emily's surprised and practiced eye, hard-to-get and unusual items, which, she also noted, didn't stay in the shop for long. On her third visit to the Bell, George Knight, the proprietor, a rotund little man with an overabundance of nervous energy, had explained the reason for this fast turnover.

He had been, as usual, meticulously dressed, if somewhat flamboyantly, and was hopping around the shop, busily flicking a feather duster over prized Limoges and Meissen, a beribboned pince-nez resting on the button nose of his cherubic face, as he'd elaborated on the whys and wherefores that such rare items should be found in such an out-of-the-way shop.

Five years earlier he'd sold his highly lucrative antique business in London and decided to retire to the south of France. But a year of travel and self-indulgence taught him that the life of the idle rich was not for him. He missed his antique world, and yet he did not want the rat race of

London again. So he compromised. He looked for and found a pleasant English village—Kingscombe fitted the bill admirably—and opened up a shop. He had excellent connections, his knowledge, his friends and acquaintances seemed never ending, and he possessed an enviable talent for tracking down specific items for commercial dealers or private collectors. Seldom was he ever unable to produce the goods required within a week or so of the initial request.

Fascinated by his stories, Emily duly related them to Sarah, who seemed delighted that her young companion had found this interest. It had been a week later, when Emily had dropped into the shop again in hopes of hearing more tales of discovery, that George Knight had asked her if she could possibly see her way clear to put in a few hours' work in the shop two or three days a week. It seemed Colonel Hawkins had asked him to catalog and set up the displays for the Victorian Toy Museum, a task that would take several weeks; since he'd be spending a great deal of time at Harewood Hall, he needed someone to take care of the shop. Delighted at the prospect, Emily consulted Sarah, who to Emily's delight gave wholehearted approval. It was decided she should work in the shop Thursday and Friday mornings and all day Saturday. All in all, the past few weeks had been some of the happiest in Emily's life.

When she entered the sunny kitchen, Mrs. Dawson was standing at the counter pouring steaming coffee into one cup, tea into another. She motioned Emily to the table.

"Sit down, dear. Thought I'd have a cup with you if you don't mind, seeing as I've been given orders to be quiet until Mrs. Loft gets out of bed," she added in an aggrieved tone.

"She's not up yet?" asked Emily, showing surprise. "That's unusual. She's always out of bed by six-thirty...."

Mrs. Dawson nodded in agreement. "I know, dear," she said, setting the cups on the table and placing a plate of toast and jar of marmalade before Emily. "But I found this note propped up on the sink when I came in." Fumbling in her coverall pocket, she extracted a folded piece of paper that she handed to Emily.

Scrawled in Sarah's unmistakable backhand were the words: "Mrs. Dawson: Please do not prepare breakfast for me as I shall be sleeping late, and I'd appreciate it if you wouldn't use the vacuum cleaner until this afternoon. Sarah Loft."

"That's odd," said Emily, sipping her coffee, "I wonder if she's out of sleeping pills?"

"Oh, I know it couldn't be that, dear," said Ruth Dawson making a grimace as Emily drank the black brew. For the life of her she couldn't understand how one could drink the beastly stuff. "I just had the prescription refilled at the chemist's yesterday." Her grimace relaxed as Emily put the cup down. "But you know," she continued, "sometimes you can take one of those little pills and still not sleep a wink. Don't know why it has that effect sometimes."

"Well, I certainly wish *I'd* had something to give me a good sleep last night," said Emily. "I had a terrible nightmare...."

At once, Mrs. Dawson was sympathetic. "Oh, you poor dear. No wonder you have a headache!"

Emily's brow formed a frown of consternation. "Well, it wouldn't have been so bad if only I'd gone to sleep after I'd woke up from that dreadful dream," she said, "but the weirdest thing happened to me."

"Really!" said Mrs. Dawson, leaning foward expectantly.

Emily, suddenly seeing the warning gleam of anticipated gossip in the kind eyes, backed off. She didn't particularly want this passed around the village. "Well, it really wasn't much. I mean, it's unusual for me, but I'm sure hundreds of others have experienced the same thing—" her frown deepened "—although I've never heard of it happening to anyone I know," she finished lamely.

Undaunted, Mrs. Dawson plunged on. "Well?" she demanded eagerly.

Emily shrugged and gave a weak laugh. Maybe it would be better to talk about it. She took a deep breath and began her story, ending with, "I could hear everything, even a motorboat in the harbor, but I couldn't move!" She stopped. She was working herself up into a highly nervous state. She squeezed her eyes shut, and inhaled deeply. Finally, she regained her composure and opened her eyes. "I guess I must have drifted off into a deep sleep and when I woke up this morning, everything was fine—except for this darn headache."

Seeing how upset Emily had become, Mrs. Dawson moved around the table and stood with an arm over Emily's shoulders.

"Well, I should think all that would be enough to give anyone a headache!" she proclaimed. "Are you absolutely sure you didn't just imagine this, dear? I mean, well, dream it, as it were?"

"No! I know I was awake, but my body just wouldn't obey my mind. Perhaps I should see a doctor?" she asked tentatively.

"Nonsense!" admonished Mrs. Dawson. "You're fit as a fiddle! Now don't go off imagining things because of this one experience. And," she continued, putting her hand on Emily's forearm, "I've just thought of something, if it will make you feel any better. I once had quite the same thing happen to me! I most certainly did," she emphasized to Emily's look of disbelief. "It was about a year ago when I was in hospital for my gall bladder. I'd told the nurse I couldn't sleep, even with those little pills they gave me—Seconal, I think they're called—looked much like the ones Mrs. Loft takes. At any rate, doctor prescribed a different pill that gave me a feeling just like you described. I could hear the nurse walking in the hall and the noises the other patients were making, but try as I might, I couldn't move or talk. Believe me, one pill was enough! After that, I never complained and was contented to stay awake!"

"But I didn't take a pill last night," said Emily.

"I know you didn't, dear," soothed Mrs. Dawson, patting Emily's arm. "I only told you about that time to show you that other people have felt the same way, but it doesn't have to be caused by medicine, I'm sure." Considering the subject closed, Mrs. Dawson began gathering the dishes.

"You didn't finish your toast," she admonished.

"I'm sorry, Mrs. Dawson, but one piece was all I could manage. If I feel better, I'll have an early lunch."

"Well, be sure you eat hearty then." *For tomorrow you shall die*, thought Emily. She shook herself. Now why should that morbid phrase pop into her head, she wondered.

"By the way, dear," said Mrs. Dawson, "were you down here in the night?"

"No, why?"

"Well, I found this saucepan, you see, soaking in the sink when I came in. Looked as if milk had been heated in it."

"Then it had to be Mrs. Loft. I heated a thermos of milk to take up with me, but I washed the pan afterward. Oh, dear," worried Emily, "I do hope she wasn't ill."

"Oh, I doubt that, dear," said Mrs. Dawson, swirling sudsy water in the dishpan. "The last thing she'd want then would be a glass of milk to curdle the stomach."

"I was thinking more of a headache," said Emily, putting her hand to her forehead.

Mrs. Dawson dried her hands. "I really don't know why you're so upset, dear. Mrs. Loft knows there's a fresh bottle of aspirin in the bathroom cabinet that I bought when I picked up her prescription. No," continued Mrs. Dawson, firmly shaking her head, "I'm sure it must have been the storm that woke her. It woke me up about midnight and I didn't get back to sleep till after two when it finally died down. . . and you know, once you wake in the night, it can take hours to get back to sleep."

Her chin resting on her hand, Emily ruminated over Mrs. Dawson's theory.

"I expect you're right," she said. "I guess I worry unnecessarily. It's just that she's so rigid in her sleeping habits. To bed at ten-thirty, up at six-thirty.'' The housekeeper had no reply. ''Mrs. Dawson, if she's not up by ten, I want you to wake her.''

Fussily, the older woman wiped her hands on her apron. ''Oh, my dear, now you know Mrs. Loft has a firm rule that no one goes into her room.''

Emily was only too aware of Sarah's idiosyncrasy. Shortly after her arrival, her hostess had confided that she could not abide the thought of anyone having access to her personal things, and therefore, she kept her bedroom locked, except at certain times when Mrs. Dawson was allowed in to clean . . . but only under the watchful eye of her employer.

''It's not that I don't trust her,'' Sarah had said, ''It's simply that I have this thing about anyone at all going into my room. That's why I keep the door locked.''

Although she considered it foolhardy on Sarah's part to lock herself in, Emily respected the not-too-subtle warning, and had never attempted to enter the bedroom.

''I'm not asking you to go in, Mrs. Dawson. Just knock on the door until you get an answer.'' She glanced at the kitchen clock. ''Good heavens, I have to fly.'' Ignoring the housekeeper's look of distress, Emily hurried toward the stairs.

She snatched up her purse and was just about to leave the house when she heard the housekeeper call. ''Miss King!''

''What is it?'' asked Emily as Mrs. Dawson bustled toward her.

''I wonder if you'd mind dropping this at the post office?'' The housekeeper withdrew an envelope from the voluminous pocket of her coverall. "A niece of mine in Plymouth is having a birthday party come Wednesday, and this is her favorite cake recipe. Unless it gets in the mail today, she won't get it in time."

"Of course." Smiling, Emily took the proffered letter. "I certainly wouldn't want her missing her favorite cake. I'll make sure it gets on its way this morning."

Stopping to adjust her scarf before the hall mirror, Emily saw the reflection of Sarah's closed bedroom door. Suddenly, without warning, her first impressions of her own bedroom that morning flashed through her mind. Unbelievingly, she went over them again. The armoire, the chair and the door.... The door to the hall had been closed, and yet she distinctly remembered leaving it open the night before. Sarah wouldn't have closed it; she couldn't manage the stairs. Suddenly a cold finger of fear ran through her. Gingerly she walked to Sarah's door and turned the knob. It was locked. But supposing, just supposing, someone had been in the house during the night. She went over to the front door. The dead bolt was still on and obviously Mrs. Dawson had found nothing amiss when she'd come in the back way that morning. Emily shook herself. She was imagining all sorts of ridiculous things, letting an upsetting night overcome common sense. The logical explanation was that a draft in the hallway had blown her door shut! Contented that at last she had thought of the obvious solution, she stepped out into the brisk morning air.

SECURE BEHIND LOCKED DOORS, Sarah Loft was dead to the world. Sunlight, shining through the crack between the heavy draperies, splayed an

CHRISTINA BLAKE   29

irregular pattern over the inert form in the bed.
Everything was neat and tidy in the room, as its
occupant liked it. The only discordant note was
to the right of the wardrobe. A pair of stout
walking shoes had left a ring of dried water
where they'd been dropped by their owner at
four o'clock that morning.

3

COLONEL HAWKINS was not enjoying his breakfast at all. His disposition in the morning was never the best, and the staff had learned to go about their duties as inconspicuously and efficiently as possible, giving him time to come to agreeable terms with the new day. Usually, this happened after a leisurely breakfast and a good cigar.

But today was different. With every passing second, the colonel was becoming more agitated at the noise emanating from beyond the French doors. Finally, fuming, he threw down his egg spoon onto the polished table, hoisted himself out of the chair, grabbed his walking stick, which he'd left propped against the wall, and waving it above his head, went storming through the open doors.

"Leeds! Franks! Confound it, stop the racket!" He stood there a moment, listening, expecting that with his bellow, peace would reign.

But the din continued.

"Leeds! Franks!" he shouted at the top of his voice, then muttered, "Blast it, where are those two?" Which was a very foolish question, as he well knew. After voicing it aloud, he looked sheepishly around to see if anyone was within earshot, for Leeds was obviously operating the mower, and Franks was by now on his way to the station to pick up the colonel's cousins, who were arriving from London. With an abrupt turn, Colonel Hawkins reentered the house, seeking out some unwary person on whom to vent his frustration. The prim and proper Miss Hawsberry, one hand balancing a tea tray and the other reaching for the door handle, was the person he came face to face with as he flung open the door of the morning room. Immune to his temper tantrums, his housekeeper was the one person on his staff who dared to approach the colonel when he was in bad humor. A tall, angular woman, Miss Hawsberry had been in his employ for several years. From the start of their relationship, she had made it quite plain that she would take no nonsense from anyone, and that, in her unwavering opinion, she considered men to be overgrown schoolboys—the colonel included.

He had often thought he would be well rid of her but, being a fair man, could truthfully find no plausible reason to fire her—other than the poor excuse that his housekeeper never hesitated to show open disapproval if he did something she considered unbefitting a man of his age and station. At present, her tightly closed mouth and steely gaze clearly showed Miss Hawsberry had decided her employer had indeed behaved in an unseemly manner.

"Oh. There you are, Miss Hawsberry," said the colonel, brought up short in his tracks, irritatingly feeling like a naughty child caught with his hand in the jam pot. "Do you know why we must have all that racket before a respectable hour of the day?"

Not in the least perturbed, his housekeeper glided past him to the table.

"So that's what all the shouting was about, is it? You know perfectly well, Colonel, this *is* a respectable hour of the day—ten-thirty—and that to get their work done, the men have to start before noon. Leeds is leaving this afternoon for three days to visit his sister, and today just happens to be the day the tree surgeons could come to cut down those four dead trees edging the south garden. If it is too noisy for you," she said, meticulously refolding a napkin and straightening a place mat, "all you have to do is close the doors to the garden and wait until Leeds is on the other side of the house. As for the chain saw, I'm afraid you shall just have to bear with it. I've brought hot tea, and I'll ask Mary to cook some fresh breakfast for you—this is stone cold—and Jenkins just brought in the mail, which has been put on your desk." Placing a folded tabloid on the table, she continued, "Here's the London paper. You can read until the eggs are ready," and with a sweeping gesture, Miss Hawsberry removed the cold breakfast and regally left the room, closing the door after her.

Throughout the dissertation, the colonel had remained submissively silent, but with the closing of the door, he gave a defiant "harumph" to the empty room. Then, with a shrug, he crossed over, closed the French windows and sat in his chair to read the paper.

Grudgingly, he had to admit it was much quieter in the room with the doors closed. He extracted a gold watch from his vest pocket. If it was on time, the train from London should be just pulling in.

The train depot at Kingscombe was as nondescript and uninviting as most country railroad stations. Only in the summer months, when gay, boisterous vacationers tumbled off the train, did it come alive, but today, when the early-morning train from London pulled in, only the three women passengers stepped out. The one with the orange curls was the first to alight, and carrying a worn and battered suitcase, she hurried into the station only to emerge a moment later through the street doors, her black-coated figure headed toward the village proper.

She was already well up the street by the time Margaret had the four suitcases out on the station platform. Elizabeth was studying the few parked cars. "It's fortunate our friend declined the offer of a lift," she said. "Shaftsbury isn't here yet." A hint of a frown furrowed the smooth-skinned brow. "I wonder where he could be? He's never been late before."

Just then, a sleek black car nosed its way into the parking area and eased to a stop. The driver, a blond young man in his early thirties, agilely alighted, looked across to the platform, then began hurriedly walking toward the two women.

"It's not Shaftsbury."

"What did you say, Elizabeth?" Margaret Cathcart was still intent on taking stock of gloves, books and other miscellaneous items in the smallest valise before the train pulled out.

"I said it's not Shaftsbury," repeated her sister.

Margaret raised her head, pushing back her hat, which had fallen over one eye. Elizabeth instinctively moved her head an inch to the right to avoid the quail feather.

"Well that goes without saying, Elizabeth! Why, they're as different as night and day!"

Elizabeth looked heavenward in exasperation.

The young man, now a few feet from them, doffed his cap to Elizabeth, "Miss Cathcart?"

"Yes. I'm Elizabeth Cathcart. This is my sister, Miss Margaret Cathcart."

The man nodded toward Margaret. "Franks, madam. The colonel asked me to meet you. Sorry I'm late."

"Not by much," said Margaret quickly before Elizabeth could comment. "We're used to Shaftsbury being early."

"Where is Shaftsbury?" queried Elizabeth. "Not ill, I hope?"

Franks smiled disarmingly, giving his face a boyish quality belying his years.

"No, Miss Cathcart. The colonel thought he was too old to drive, so now he spends most of his time polishing the cars and puttering about." In one motion, Franks picked up two of the suit-cases and started walking toward the car, the women following on his heels. The chauffeur opened the rear door for them, but Margaret opened the front and settled herself in the passenger seat, as Franks went to retrieve the rest of the luggage.

"I'll ride up here, Elizabeth. That way Franks can give me all the news." As the car pulled out into the roadway, she could feel her sister's predictable look of displeasure burning into the back of her neck. Elizabeth would never understand that England had left the Victorian era far behind. . .or perhaps it's just me, thought Margaret. But whichever, she herself took a person for who, not what, he was, and she instinctively liked this young man.

Conversation, however, was apparently not

one of Franks's strong points, and after a stilted
comparison of London and Devon weather, he
fell into silence—much to Margaret's disppoint-
ment. Not at all like Shaftsbury, she thought,
who constantly babbled. If she were alone, she
would have asked a few pointed questions, but
Elizabeth's presence squelched the urge, so she
lapsed into her own thoughts, while Franks concentrated on his driving. And this was just as
well, for suddenly, not fifty feet ahead of them,
a black horse vaulted a low stone wall, galloped
across the road, jumped a three-foot hedge and
raced up the hill toward a stately Georgian
house. The rider didn't even glance backward as
Franks applied the brakes, deftly swerved and
drew the car to a halt. For a few seconds, no one
said anything.

Franks found his voice first. "Are you both all
right?" he asked, looking at a pale Elizabeth in
the rearview mirror.

Margaret, adjusting her hat, ignored the question. "Did you see that, Elizabeth? Did you see
that?" she asked excitedly. "It was Marion Bundy. What on earth does she think she's doing? We
could have all been killed! I'm going to ring her
up as soon as we reach the Hall."

But Elizabeth, one hand still braced against the
seat in front of her, could not find her tongue.

"Must have a death wish," offered Franks,
shaking his head.

"Well, at the moment, she certainly has *my*
death wish," fumed Margaret. She looked back
at her sister. "Are you sure you're all right, Elizabeth?"

"Yes...yes, I'm not hurt. Although I don't
think I'll ever be the same again!"

"What on earth do you think possessed her?" asked Margaret, turning to face front again. "She's usually far from careless."

"Who's to say?" sighed Elizabeth. "Perhaps life has caught up with her, and Franks is right. After all she has had a fairly miserable life."

"Oh, I don't think Marion would have a death wish," said Margaret. "No matter how miserable her life has been. And as far as that goes, I really don't think she's been so miserable. *I* certainly wouldn't be if I owned Redwing—one of the best stud farms in England—and had spent years traveling around the world!"

"Yes, but you forget the reason she traveled, Margaret," interjected Elizabeth. "If you had had what you thought was a loving husband, and then one day he just disappeared . . . along with the barmaid at the Fox and Hound—"

"Hearsay!" snapped her sister. "About the barmaid, I mean. Besides, with Marion's looks and figure, I'm sure she could have had another husband before now if she'd wanted. Even our cousin Charles, I suppose. They're certainly good friends." Margaret shook her head. "No, Elizabeth, if anyone's to blame for her solitary state, it's Marion herself. She's made her own loneliness."

But as Franks started the car, Elizabeth, now completely undaunted by his presence and trying to make her sister see her point, still pressed on.

"Be reasonable, Margaret. There was her father, remember? Did you ever meet a more austere man? Can you imagine what it must have been like to have been raised by a man who made no secret that he'd wanted a son? Why, he even spelled Marion's name with an 'o' instead of an 'a'! Imagine, then, to have to nurse him after that stroke...." Elizabeth shivered. "He certainly must have made her life miserable."

Margaret partially conceded. "You're right, Elizabeth. He was a horrible man. But surely there must have been some love there for her to come home at his bidding." She thought a minute. "How long did she nurse him, do you remember?"

"About six months, I believe," said Elizabeth.

"Three," corrected Franks.

In surprise, the two sisters looked at the chauffeur, whose ear tips turned pink. A charming trait, Margaret thought— "How do you know that?" she asked.

Franks was reluctant. "I...er...I'm sorry, Miss Cathcart. I shouldn't have been listening. I don't want to get anyone in trouble," he said.

"You won't," said Margaret. Under her direct gaze, Franks's ears turned even pinker.

Finally he blurted, "It was Grace Dawson who told me."

"Grace Dawson?"

"Yes. She takes care of the house for Mrs. Bundy. She's lived here all her life."

"And so she gossips about her employer," said Elizabeth primly, once more wrapped in her Victorian cocoon.

"Oh, stop it, Elizabeth," said Margaret, although not unkindly. "For goodness' sake, there's no reason Grace can't talk about Marion. There's certainly enough to say," she tagged on. She turned back to Franks. "I'd like to meet your Grace," she said in an effort to soothe over Elizabeth's retort. "I imagine she's a lovely girl."

To Franks's relief, no answer was required, for

at that moment they drove between the stone entrance pillars to Harewood Hall, and both women instantly became absorbed in more immediate issues.

The colonel was about to light a cigar when he saw the car rolling up the driveway. Confound it! Everyone was on schedule today except him! Although anxious to see his cousins, he'd hoped to have a chance to enjoy his daily luxury of one cigar and then thoroughly air the room before they arrived. Elizabeth never could abide cigar smoke. Heaving a sigh of disappointment, he carefully placed the cheroot in his breast pocket and went out to greet Elizabeth and Margaret.

As he hastily adjusted his cravat before the hall mirror, the glass reflected a tall straight figure, with a white mane of hair flowing back from a high forehead, a prominent jaw, softened by the thickness that comes with age, and blue eyes, somewhat distilled, set below bushy white brows. All in all, he had fared well for a man in his mid-sixties.

Franks was just bringing the Mercedes to a halt as the colonel opened the door. Waving to the two smiling faces, he marveled how three such entirely different people, both in looks and temperament, could have the same grandparents. The only thing the colonel and his two cousins had in common was that they had never married—although he'd come close to it once. As for Elizabeth, he felt sure she had never had the time nor the opportunity to consider matrimony. Life had treated her, if not cruelly, then unfairly, leaving her motherless at sixteen to raise a lively young sister, then between them care for an invalid father. Her burden had given her some-

thing neither he nor his other cousin possessed:
an unquenchable tolerance for others.

The front door on the other side of the car flew
open and his other cousin scrambled out. The colonel smiled. Margaret was single simply because
she was Margaret. Although eleven years younger
than her sister, she was definitely the more dom-
inant of the two. Unlike Elizabeth, she had no
patience or finesse, but she had plenty of determination, stubbornness and aggressiveness. Not
unattractive in face and figure, she wore exactly
what she liked, matched or mismatched and
somehow never flattering.

Was ever a man born who could control her,
wondered the colonel, as he moved agilely over
to the other side of the porch to avoid being
speared by the quail feather.

"Well, Charles, seems as though the weather
will be kind to you for your party tonight. Let's
hope it keeps up for the grand opening," said
Margaret, giving him a hefty bear hug and a
nudge on the arm. Wincing, for Margaret's nudges
were never light, the colonel took her valise and,
putting his arm around her shoulders, turned to
greet his other cousin. "Charles! You should
have seen—" began Margaret.

"Charles, dear," said Elizabeth hastily, throwing her sister a quelling look while proffering her
cheek for her cousin's greeting. "It's so good to
see you again! And isn't the weather glorious!
We had a terrible storm in London last night, but
thank goodness it had let up by this morning or
we'd never have made it."

"Well, you're here now," said Charles, leading
them inside, "and you can have a nice long nap
today. Did you breakfast on the train?"

His question opened up the subject of train food, finally concluded by Margaret's, "Personally, I'm ready for a good strong cup of tea and a decent breakfast."

"I don't blame you a bit," chuckled the colonel. "Just leave your things here in the hall, then go into the morning room and ring for Hawsberry. In fact, knowing her, she probably has an ample breakfast set out for you already. I'll join you shortly. Have to see Leeds about something."

The colonel had not been mistaken about his housekeeper. Entering the dining room, Margaret and Elizabeth found two places set at the small table by the window and Miss Hawsberry transferring food from a tray onto plates.

"Good morning, Miss Elizabeth, Miss Margaret," she said, with a nod to each of them. "Thought you'd like something substantial when you arrived. I know how those trains are."

"Miss Hawsberry, you are a gem," said Margaret, helping herself to buttered toast. "Any time you'd like to leave our cousin and come live in London...."

The housekeeper smiled. "Thank you, Miss Margaret, and don't be surprised if I accept that offer some day. The colonel's getting more irascible all the time," she said. "Now I must see about the sausages and eggs, so you and Miss Elizabeth tuck into the berries and I'll be back in a moment." This last bit of advice was superfluous for Margaret, who was already doing justice to the fruit.

Three quarters of an hour later, after Elizabeth retired to her room for a nap and Margaret was sitting on the terrace, Charles Hawkins returned.

"Ah! I see Hawsberry took good care of you,"

he said, spying the dishes. "Where's Elizabeth?"

"Gone upstairs for a rest. She's feeling the effects of getting up so early this morning to catch the train. Odd, but it doesn't seem to have hit me yet."

The colonel snorted and said, "I don't expect it will, Margaret. You always were quite tireless." Pouring himself a cup of tea from the pot on the sideboard and sitting in the wicker chair opposite, he said, "Well, now, you and I can have a nice chat . . . and I'll enjoy the cigar I missed this morning. Do you mind?" He reached for his breast pocket.

"No, of course not. Now's a good time with Elizabeth resting."

"Right. Sorry I took so long," he apologized, "but I wanted to remind Leeds to be sure to put a padlock on the door to the greenhouse before he leaves to visit his sister. A few nights ago, some vandals broke into the conservatory at Redwing. Smashed and trampled most of the flowers, slashed bags of fertilizer, smashed pots . . . everything was strewn about. Never had anything like that happen before."

"Good heavens!" exclaimed Margaret. "Did they catch anyone?"

"No," said Charles, puffing deeply on his cigar. "Police put it down to early summer visitors out for mischief, since there seemed no rhyme or reason for it. About a hundred pounds' worth of damage, though. Marion Bundy was quite upset about it."

Margaret smiled wryly. "I'll bet she was. All she ever talks about are her horses and flowers."

Charles grunted in assent and tapped cigar ash into the ashtray. "Ordinarily, I wouldn't think of

locking up the greenhouse, but now that this has
happened, I'll sleep better knowing my prize
blooms are under lock and key.''

"I don't doubt it, and I'll sleep better, too,"
said Margaret. "By the way, Charles, while I
think of it, I like the new chauffeur."

"Franks? Yes," said her cousin, nodding, "he's
a good man. Had him about two months. Quite
amiable and certainly handy with tools. Marion's
always had difficulty finding a good mechanic
for her Mercedes, and she was complaining the
other day about something or other acting up."
He sipped his tea. "I asked Franks to have a look
at it. Had it fixed in no time. I dare say, Marion
wishes she had him in her employ," chuckled
Charles, "but I'm not about to give him up, and I
can't deny it's a pleasure to have someone driving whose reflexes I can rely on. Poor old Shaftsbury would get rattled every time we went past
the gates."

"I hope he isn't bored," said Margaret.

"No, he's quite happy, living his life out in our
tranquil little village."

Margaret looked at him from under lowered
lids. "It must be the season," she said. "You're
the second one who's told me that today."

"What?" said the confused colonel. "You
mean about Shaftsbury?"

"No, no! Not Shaftsbury! I'm speaking of your
reference to the village being tranquil. A woman
on the train was complaining that nothing exciting ever happens in the country."

"Margaret," said Charles patiently, "you know
as well as I do that life in Kingscombe goes on
much the same from one day to the next. What
happened at Redwing was terribly out of character."

"You think that, Charles, but then you do tend to hide your head in the sand," said Margaret. "Human nature does *not* go on the same from day to day. Strong emotions are often buried, and it only takes a word in the wrong place to set them on a rampage sometimes."

"Margaret," said Charles placidly, "we are talking of a very small village—not the city of London."

Spreading her arms, as if to encompass the whole village, Margaret continued to pound home her point. "Here, my dear Charles, you have a miniature London. Oh, yes, you have," she said, when her cousin scoffed. "Only instead of several thousand of a kind, you have one or two...but just as great a variety of people, and I'll bet if some of these old buildings could talk, we'd hear a lot of juicy tales." A contented feline smile played at the corners of her mouth. "In fact, I wouldn't be surprised if there's been a murder or two with skeletons sealed up in walls."

"Well, I'm afraid you're in for a disappointment, my girl," said Charles. "Our 'Londoners' are quite a common-garden variety—no rare specimens."

Margaret threw up her hands in exasperation. "Oh, Charles! How can you possibly be so blind?"

But the colonel was not to be drawn. There was a long, not uncomfortable silence while he puffed heavily on his cigar, and Margaret sat with eyes closed, her face uplifted toward the sun.

Finally, bored with the silence, and still determined to bring her cousin around to her way of thinking, Margaret asked in a deceptively innocent voice, "Tell me, Charles, is Kingscombe still blessed with Potty Purdy?"

The question had the desired effect. Charles

almost bit right through his cigar. "Margaret!
You don't go around calling a vicar 'potty'! And
anyway, he's not—potty, I mean. 'Eccentric,'
perhaps. After all, we all of us have our little ec-
centricities," he reasoned.

Margaret sat up with a snap and pointed an ac-
cusing finger at Charles. "There! I told you so!"
she triumphed. "We all have little, harmless ec-
centricities, yes, Charles. But we certainly don't
go around looking for evil the way he does." The
colonel opened his mouth to protest, but hastily
closed it as Margaret went on, "If anyone can
find maleficence in innocence, he can." She gave
her cousin a defiant look. "And stop defending
him. He *is* potty," said Margaret with finality.

To argue with his cousin when she used that
tone of voice was fruitless, as Charles well knew,
but the short discussion of Reverend Purdy had
brought to mind a bit of news that, although not
exactly exciting, did change the subject. "There
is something of interest that's happened since
you were here last."

"Ah ha! I knew it!" said Margaret elatedly.

Slowly and with agonizing deliberateness,
Charles got up to pour himself another cup of
tea, determined to begin his story in his own
good time.

"Well?" prompted Margaret impatiently.

"Patience, dear Margaret." After her biting
remarks, he was thoroughly enjoying her discomfort. He stirred in sugar, walked back to his chair
and sat down. "Now," he said, settling himself
in, "we have two new people in Kingscombe;
you'll be meeting them tonight. One is Mrs. Sarah
Loft and the other, Miss Emily King." Immediately, Margaret opened her mouth, but before

she could interject any question, he hurried on. "You'll like Emily King. . .sweet young thing. . . visiting here from Canada. She's done a few minor repairs on the museum exhibits. Has fine hands and knows how to use them. At present, she's repairing one of our dolls—beautiful bisque head, but the kid body is in a sorry state. However, if anyone can do anything with it, Emily can. She's on leave from her Canadian job, where she's an assistant curator for a museum. I don't know how George Knight would have managed without her—you see she helps out in the shop when he's down at the coach house. As for the other newcomer. . . ." The colonel paused for emphasis, seeing he had his cousin's full attention. "As for the other one, Margaret," he said slowly and wagging a finger at her, "you'd better be on your guard! She's a true match for you. She's a writer, and if you think you have an inquiring mind, wait until you meet her! I swear Sarah Loft could ferret information from a sphinx." Shaking his head in wonderment, he continued. "Even I didn't realize, until long after our conversation ended, that she'd been pumping me, and by that time, I wasn't at all sure what I *did* tell her!" He chuckled delightedly. "I don't know if she's done it to anyone else in the village, but I will say, she's certainly a smart one!" The colonel sat back, arms folded across his chest. "Yes," he said, as much to himself as to his cousin, "You're going to have to be razor-sharp with this one, Margaret." He puffed contentedly on his cigar, anticipating the inevitable meeting of these two strong-minded women.

Margaret's reaction was not what he anticipated. "Wonderful!" she said, clapping her

hands with glee, not in the least ruffled by
Charles's dire predictions. "It sounds like an exciting evening ahead, and as the old saying goes,
'Forewarned is forearmed.'" She leaned forward
in her seat. "What brought her to Kingscombe?"

"Hmm?" Charles hated to be brought back
from his dream of seeing his cousin meet her
Waterloo. "Oh, sorry, Margaret, what was that?"

"I said, Charles, why did this Sarah Loft come
to Kingscombe?"

"Oh, primarily for her health, I think. I understand her doctor said she needed the sea air.
Lives in Rose Hill cottage... don't know whether
you recall it... lovely house... fifteenth century... at the top of the road... white, with blue
shutters...?" At Margaret's nod and impatient
gesture to get on with it, he hurriedly resumed to
the point of the question. "Yes. Well, old Mr.
Wridgley died and the estate put it up for sale.
Sarah's nephew, who's a barrister in London—
you'll meet him too, by the way, since he'll be
here tonight. Nice young chap... family's from
'round Dartmouth way.... I think he's rather
sweet on Emily...."

"For goodness' sake, Charles, please stick to
the subject," said his cousin irritably.

Charles blinked. "Oh, sorry. Where was I?"

Margaret heaved a sigh. "The nephew..." she
said resignedly.

"Oh, yes. John Trask. Well, he saw the place,
and negotiations were completed then and there.
Understand he paid on the spot." The colonel
chortled. "I'll bet old Wridgley sat up in his grave
when the money exchanged hands! Now there
was a moneygrabber for you!"

Margaret held up her hand to ward off any further deviation from the main subject. "When did she move in?"

"Oh, very soon after I think. The real-estate agents had modernized it and decorated before putting it up for sale, so it was all ready for immediate occupancy. That was about the end of February. Then Emily arrived several weeks ago. Seems she and Sarah have a mutual friend in Canada."

"Charles, listen," said Margaret. "You said she's a writer. What does she write?"

The colonel sat back in his chair and beamed. He'd been waiting for this one. "I've no idea," he said.

"What do you mean, you've no idea? Haven't you asked her?" said Margaret.

"Of course, I have," said her cousin, "and all I could get out of her was something about the stories not being of interest to me."

"But that's ridiculous! I've never heard of such a thing. A writer who doesn't publicize her writing?"

"I couldn't agree more. I told you she was an odd one!"

"Where's she from? What's her background?" demanded his cousin.

"She's from London, and she writes. That's all I know."

"Do you mean to tell me, Charles, that with all the gossip that goes on around here, there's nothing else to say about a newcomer in the village?"

"Believe me," said Charles, "Sarah Loft does not give out any information she doesn't want to! Two of a kind you are." He rubbed his palms together in anticipation. "Perhaps I should charge for tonight's performance. Oh, I *am* going to enjoy it!''

''Charles, it may deflate you a little,'' said Margaret sweetly, ''but I, for one, am looking forward to making her acquaintance, so stop your braying, and while we're on the subject of this evening, who else is going to be here?''

''Just a few friends to celebrate the museum opening. Unfortunately, George Knight can't come. There's an estate auction that evidently has some rare items going and he feels he shouldn't miss it. If he gets back early enough, he'll join us. It's going to make us a bit lopsided as far as more women than men, but it can't be helped.''

''Who'll be here?'' repeated Margaret, getting her cousin back on the main track.

''Well,'' said Charles, ticking them off on his fingers, ''there's you, Elizabeth and I, Richard and Amy Purdy, Emily King, Sarah Loft and her nephew, John Trask, Fred Cotes—his wife is in bed with the flu so she can't come—Alicia Rochmere and Marion Bundy.'' Noting his cousin's grimace, he rushed on to say, ''Now, Margaret, I want you to behave. Marion has donated the pièce de résistance to our little museum. A mid-nineteenth-century dollhouse, fully furnished to the last detail, containing a solid-gold miniature serving set for six . . . and believe me, it's insured for a packet.''

''It sounds like Marion Bundy,'' snorted Margaret. ''Let someone instigate an idea and do all the hard work, then she'll come up with all the glory. You know, Charles, she has an overbearing way I find difficult to tolerate.''

''Nonsense. Marion has never hurt anyone.''

''Well, I don't like her.''

"Personally," said Charles, a twinkle in his eye, "I think it's the old green-eyed monster on your part."

"You couldn't be more wrong, dear cousin," said Margaret, and picking up her cardigan, she walked over to the edge of the terrace to lean on the low stone wall, her back to her cousin. "I don't envy her lonely life, and as for money . . . I have enough to suffice. No," she continued, shaking her head, "it's just that somehow I don't trust her."

"But that's ridiculous!" blustered the colonel. "I've known her all my life. We were children together . . . and I can tell you, Marion has always been a model of decorum."

"Model of decorum or not, just remember, Charles, dear, the age-old saying, 'Still waters run deep.' I don't think Marion Bundy has ever let anyone see the bottom of the river bed."

"Well, I think you're making a mountain out of a molehill," said her cousin. "And please, Margaret, do try not to be too blunt with Marion tonight."

Turning to face him, Margaret made a mock salute. "Charles, you have my solemn promise I shall not embarrass you tonight. Believe me, I shall be the model of decorum myself." Then, as the thought popped into her head, she asked, "By the way, just out of curiosity, what does our friend Marion think of Sarah Loft?"

Charles shrugged. "As far as I know, they've never met."

"My, my," said Margaret. "It truly is going to be an interesting evening! Charles, be a dear and seat Sarah Loft next to Marion, with me across the table. From the sound of it, this new villager could put our Mrs. Bundy in her place; after all, if I'm going to be giving you a show, I think it only fair that I see one, too. And now I'm going to change. I think, Charles, I shall pay a visit to the Bell. It wouldn't hurt to meet Emily King before tonight. And," she added, as she turned to go, "who says nothing much ever happens here? Tonight promises to be quite exciting. I'm truly looking foward to meeting my opponent!"

MARGARET WASN'T THE ONLY ONE looking forward to meeting new faces. While she changed, Sarah Loft sat before her dressing table, speculating about the evening's party. She'd been in Kingscombe for three months, and time was running out.

Looking about the room, she mentally took stock. Any signs of last night's activity had been meticulously removed. Shoes had been polished and safely put away and the water mark carefully eradicated. Now, however, other tools of her trade had been laid out—strange tools, that would give Mrs. Dawson cause for fright if she knew they were there.

4

ALICIA ROCHMERE HAD COMPOSED HERSELF from the morning's shock. She had put the calamity out of her head—it really was too painful to think about—at least for today. She knew who the culprit was, and she would deal with him later.

At precisely eleven-thirty, her spare figure clad in a slightly worn blue coat, subdued navy print dress, highly polished blue shoes, and small navy straw hat—an attire she judged proper for a lady going to market—she stepped out her front door locking it behind her and dropping the key into her purse. It was when she turned to begin her descent to the walkway that she noticed the parcel sitting at the edge of the top step. She went over to take a closer look.

The box was about nine inches square, wrapped in brown paper and tied with white string. Had Jenkins, the postman, accidentally dropped it while on his morning round? Gingerly picking it up at the knot, she held it between thumb and forefinger and saw that there was no postmark; obviously it hadn't come in the mail. Pasted on one side, in block letters, was her name, MISS A. ROCHMERE. That was all. No address, not any clue as to who had left it, was evident. Strange. She shook it and couldn't hear a thing. Maybe it was another prank, she thought;

then again, maybe it wasn't. Bother! She stamped her foot in irritation. Such things never failed to happen when one was in a hurry—although in truth, Alicia Rochmere was rarely ever rushed. But today was an exception. The colonel's dinner party was tonight, and she still had lots to do before seven o'clock. To put this package into the house would mean using precious moments to hunt around in her bag for the key and unlock the door. A nuisance, she thought...yet she could hardly leave the thing here in plain sight. So since it wasn't heavy, nor very large, she did the only thing she could think of on the spur of the moment. She popped it into her shopping bag and set off for the village.

IT WAS NOON, and Emily sat at the desk in the workroom of the antique shop, attempting to do some paper work. But try as she might, her mind just wouldn't concentrate on facts and figures, and what was more, she couldn't rid herself of a feeling of apprehension. Just what she was apprehensive about, she couldn't say...but there was something. It wasn't Sarah. Since she hadn't heard from Mrs. Dawson, she knew her hostess must be all right, but several times during the morning the housekeeper's story of her own strange experience with a sleeping pill filtered through her thoughts. The more she tried to disregard it, the more persistent it became, and finally, in disgust, she threw the pen down onto the desk blotter.

It was no use. She couldn't concentrate on anything. Even the wooden crate that had been delivered that morning hadn't had the power to induce her to take an interest in her work. She glanced at the object in question. The truth was she really wasn't too sure whether or not she should open it. Up until now, all special orders had been delivered when George Knight was there to receive them. He would promptly open and inspect them.

This purchase was supposed to have been delivered to the shop in the afternoon. Emily had distinctly heard her employer give specific orders to the van lines at the docks when he called to inform them a crate would be ready for pickup at the customs office. What no one had planned on was the shipment being handled by an overeager customs officer and an equally industrious truck driver, resulting in the box from the hold of the Lebanese ship being delivered to the shop that morning. She knew what the crate contained—a small, veneered lady's table, inlaid with delicate porcelain plaques and signed by a well-known French *ébéniste*. Ever since Mr. Knight had told her he'd tracked it down in a private collection, Emily had impatiently awaited its arrival; but now, with the past night's anxieties weighing heavily on her, the delivery of the antiquity was somehow anticlimactic.

Pushing her chair back, she got up and went over to the coatrack. Perhaps if she got some air, it would help clear her head and make her feel more like working this afternoon. Besides, George Knight would probably be in when she got back from lunch. She put on her coat and scarf and flipped the sign hanging on the door to read Closed.

Outside, the warm breeze of the morning was no longer gentle, but had worked its way up to a

chill, biting wind. Making her way to the sea
wall, things didn't seem quite so ominous. Emily
drew in a deep breath of salt air. Obviously, the
seed implanted by Mrs. Dawson had outgrown all
proportion. The idea of being...what?...
drugged?...was absolutely ridiculous! She'd had
a nightmare and that was that!

Suddenly she smiled. In a few hours she'd be
with John, all ready for the evening's festivities.
A warm feeling of anticipation flowed through
her. Life had become lovely once again. Aware-
ness of the present also made her realize she was
hungry.

Since she had closed the shop a half hour
earlier than usual, she decided to pick up something sinfully fattening for herself and eat it back
at the Bell, rather than stop at the tea shop for
lunch.

With a spring to her step, she made her way
toward the bakery, planning the rest of her day
as she walked. Pick up Mr. Knight's pastry order,
then perhaps leave work a little early so she
could have a short nap before dressing for the
party...and John. But Emily's plans for Saturday went completely awry.

THE CROWD of morning shoppers had dwindled
considerably when Emily entered Nottingham's
Bakery, and the proprietress, her round face
wreathed in smiles, came scurrying from the
back room. "Miss King!" she said. "How are you
and Mrs. Loft?"

"Fine, thank you," said Emily. Mrs. Nottingham was one of these people who exude
warmth. Her blond hair, plaited and coiled
around her head, combined with rosy cheeks and

blue twinkling eyes, always made Emily think of a Mrs. Santa Claus.

"What can we do for you, now?" she asked Emily.

"I know I'm a bit early," said Emily, "but I came to pick up Mr. Knight's Saturday order."

"Oh, I am sorry, Miss King, but it's not quite ready. We're all behind today. My young assistant rang up this morning to say he's got the flu and I've had to double up with the baking and looking after the shop. But it won't be more than five minutes before Mr. Knight's order is ready. I'll get right to it."

"Oh," said Emily, "will you add a pineapple cream-and-custard tart to the order for me, please?"

The older woman beamed. "Treating ourselves today, are we? With your figure you can certainly stand it," she said. "I won't be but a few minutes."

Every Saturday Emily picked up pastries for George Knight. When he came in the afternoon, after spending the morning at the coach house, he did the week's bookkeeping while drinking tea and eating the cakes.

At last Mrs. Nottingham pushed her abundant frame through the doorway from the kitchen, carrying a plate of cakes wrapped in white paper and tied with a string, as well as a smaller, paper-wrapped package containing Emily's order. "Here we are now."

Reaching into her purse for money, Emily spied Mrs. Dawson's letter. Good heavens! She'd forgotten all about it! Well, if she mailed it now, it would still go out that day. She paid the modest sum and made her way next door.

The village post office never ceased to fasci-
nate Emily. Accustomed to the efficient but bar-
ren post offices in Canada, the idea of a little
cage tucked away in the corner of a shop that
sold everything from A to Z delighted her. One
could spend days here, she thought, and still not
know half the stock. Letting her eyes travel
along one shelf behind the counter, she saw
bolts of colorful material, sewing notions, dart
boards, soccer balls, boxes of candy, a cardboard box filled with what looked like small
plastic toy cars, a few tins of peas, several
wheels of gaily colored ribbon, and wedged between the ribbon and wall were packages of tea.
Every shelf was cluttered and packed to such an
extent that items had to be requested rather
than sought out. The counter, running the full
length of the shop, was just as overflowing with
merchandise as the shelves behind, except for
the small glass-enclosed section designated as
government property. Standing just inside the
door were racks of slightly soiled post cards and
greeting cards, while suspended from the ceiling
were bright beach balls and multicolored pails
and shovels.

Behind the counter on a high stool sat the
mistress of this maze, Miss Joyce Twickham. Her
homely face broke into a smile when she saw
Emily enter.

"What can I do for you, Miss King?"

"I'd just like a stamp, please," said Emily.

"Overseas?" asked the postmistress, who was
well acquainted with Emily's correspondence.

"No, regular. I have a letter to mail for Mrs.
Dawson," Emily replied following the tall,
rather ungainly woman along the other side of

the counter toward the post-office cubicle. A display of colored glass caught her eye. "Oh, how pretty! Are these new?" she asked, stopping midway along the counter.

Miss Twickham looked back to where Emily was standing. "Oh, those? Yes, it's a new delivery, but I always have them in stock. Those just arrived yesterday. Some of them are unusual, aren't they?"

"I've never seen any as pretty as these," said Emily, pulling a multifaceted green one out of the Styrofoam. Holding it up, she watched the light play through it. "But I didn't know these long hatpins were in fashion again."

"Well, they aren't really in fashion as hatpins, but a lot of young girls buy them to dress up their long hair. You know, they twist it up and then stick a few of these around it. It really is quite attractive. Of course, they have to file down the point first. It would be rather dangerous if they didn't."

"I expect so," agreed Emily with a laugh; then, examining the pins again, she picked up a lavender one. "This lavender pin is pretty, too," she said, comparing the two, "but no, I think I'll take the green . . . and anyway, it will look nice as a lapel pin on my navy suit."

"I never thought of using it like that," said Miss Twickham, counting out Emily's change and handing her the stamp. "I do like a girl who can improvise."

Just then a movement of the red curtains that separated the living quarters from the store caught Emily's attention. A woman with bright orange curls emerged from between the draperies. "How much are these bathing caps?" she asked without so much as a glance in Emily's direction.

"Oh, Flora. Didn't I put them on the list?"

"No you didn't," whined the petulant nasal voice.

"I'll take care of it right now, dear," soothed the postmistress. Then, feeling her manners were remiss, she said, "Miss King, I'd like you to meet my cousin, Flora Wickes, who arrived this morning."

The orange curls gave an indifferent nod to Emily's, "How do you do?"

"Will you be here long?" asked Emily more out of politeness than curiosity.

"Few days," came the curt reply.

"Till Tuesday," filled in Miss Twickham. "She's going to mind the store while I go galavanting to a wedding. I'll be home late Tuesday evening."

"Are you going far?" asked Emily.

"Quite a way," said the postmistress. "A little place near Durham—Waltham Dale, to be exact. I was born there, and I'm going to the wedding of the daughter of a dear friend of mine. I'll be catching this evening's train to London, then I'll change trains there."

"Oh," said Emily. "I assumed you were from around here."

Miss Twickham laughed. "Well, I feel as though I've lived here all my life, but in truth I've only been here for the past twelve years. I don't get back up north very often. This shop keeps me so busy I've no time for holidays. In fact, I haven't gone anywhere in the past three years, so I feel I'm due a few days off."

"How did you end up in Kingscombe?" asked Emily.

"A friend of mine in Waltham Dale told me about this place, and—"

"The one whose daughter is getting married?"

"Good heavens, no. The friend who told me about Kingscombe died last year."

"Oh, I'm sorry," said Emily.

"I shall miss seeing her when I go back. Not that we were really that close, mind. We belonged to the same church circle, and worked together at several bazaars and socials. Anyway, we moved south because of my mother's health. Her doctor recommended a kinder climate. Since she died several years ago, I've thought more than once about moving back to old haunts. . . ."

A none-too-discreet cough from Flora reminded the postmistress of her neglected duty.

"Will you excuse me, Miss King, while I see to the bathing caps?" said Miss Twickham. And parting the curtains, she steered her cousin through the opening.

"Well, I wish you a pleasant journey. We'll miss you around here," called Emily, gathering her parcels.

"Oh, is someone going somewhere?" whispered a voice at her ear. Emily almost jumped out of her skin. The chilling figure of the vicar was standing directly behind her.

Elongated. That was the best word to describe the Reverend Purdy. Not tall. Elongated. . . as if some power had taken him by the hair and stretched an average, evenly proportioned five-foot frame ten or eleven inches, narrowing the shoulders and hips, resulting in a too-thin cadaverous-looking body, over which the gray skin appeared strained nearly beyond the point of elasticity. His face, with its hooked nose, hollowed cheeks and sunken eyes, rarely showed any expression other than a rapid blinking of the eyes when excited. This could be very disconcerting for anyone in his presence at such a time, for one found oneself involuntarily imitating this mannerism.

"Reverend Purdy! I didn't hear you come in," exclaimed Emily, her heart resuming its normal speed.

"No, not many people do, my child, and it's most unfortunate. I'm here to help all—" he heaved a sigh "—but few will let me into their hearts and souls. And I am sorry. Most assuredly I didn't mean to frighten you."

"Oh, I wouldn't say you frightened me," she lied. "A more appropriate word would be 'startled.'" Before he could reply to that, the red drapes parted and the sunken gray eyes shifted to that direction.

"Well, good afternoon, vicar," said Miss Twickham, coming into the room. "Lovely day, isn't it? Wind's bit chilly, though."

"Yes. Yes it is. I thought perhaps last night, however, that the good Lord had given up on all us sinners and declared another forty days and nights."

"Oh, I don't think we need worry about that. As it says in the Bible—Revelations, I believe— when God destroys the world, it will be by fire, not by water," said Miss Twickham smoothly, and immediately could have bitten her tongue.

"Eh? Well, yes, *I* know that, Miss Twickham," said the vicar, who had turned slightly pink at the idea of someone correcting him in his own

bailiwick, "but the Lord also moves in mysterious ways," he continued, wagging a bony
finger in front of the postmistress's nose. "However, perhaps he was giving us fair warning with
last night's display of thunder and lightning. You
know as well as I do, dear lady, that the
devil . . . yes the devil, is at work in all of us. . . ."

Emily, seeing they might be in for one of
Reverend Purdy's long, impromptu and by all
means boring sermons, began inching her way
toward the door.

". . . eating away at our insides, and if I can
help even a few of those innocents, who have
not yet seen the light, and realize that they
possess Him within their bodies, then I shall feel I
have done God's will on earth." This last was
said with head bowed and eyes closed.

Knowing from past experience that one way to
stop the vicar when he was on one of his tirades
was to flatter him, Miss Twickham soothed,
"And you're doing fine work, Reverend Purdy.
Your sermon last Sunday was inspirational. I'm
sure you sent many parishioners home contemplating your words of wisdom." Deftly, her
thumbnail slit the seal of a cardboard box. "But
really, I must get on with my work. You save the
souls and I'll save the store, eh? Now, did you
want anything?"

Richard Purdy's head snapped up and his eyes
blinked rapidly. "As a matter of fact, Miss
Twickham, I want to talk to you." Leaning across
the counter and speaking in a conspiratorial
tone, but purposely loud enough for Emily to
hear, he said, "The devil, you see, is at work in
Kingscombe. I've just reported a crime to the
police."

Emily stopped in her tracks.

His bombshell had the desired effect and Miss Twickham, in the process of stacking bars of chocolate on the already overburdened shelf instantly paused, her hand holding a burnt-almond bar, poised in midair. "A crime!" she ejaculated. "Here in Kingscombe?"

"I don't believe it!" said Emily, joining the other two at the counter.

"What sort of crime?" asked Miss Twickham, and then, realizing she still held the bar of chocolate, hastily put it down.

"The crime, my dear ladies," said the vicar, blossoming before his audience, "is thievery."

"No!" interjected Miss Twickham.

The vicar nodded his head. "When I went into our church this morning, I discovered that two of the brass candlesticks and a chalice were missing."

"But that's terrible!" exclaimed the postmistress. "Who would want to rob a church?"

"Who indeed, Miss Twickham," said the vicar dryly. "But unfortunately, it seems to be the thing to do these days. Just last week one of the Catholic churches nearby was robbed of three vestments. Obviously, one has to conclude that, since a vestment would be of use only to a man of the Cloth, *that* robbery was done through spite. On the other hand, however, the motive for stealing our candlesticks and chalice was probably monetary."

"But do you have any idea when this robbery took place?" asked Miss Twickham.

"Ah!" said the Reverend Purdy, this time pointing the bony forefinger heavenward, "now

that is precisely what I want to talk to you about.
I was hoping, you see, that perhaps you might
have seen something.''

"Me?" Miss Twickham said, aghast. "But when
would I have seen anything?"

"Oh, my dear Miss Twickham," said the vicar,
rubbing his palms together and gloating with glee
at the information he was about to reveal, "last
night of course or rather, shall we say, ap-
proximately three this morning," he said, arch-
ing a thin eyebrow. "When you were with that
man!"

Miss Twickham turned beet red.

Now he's gone too far, thought Emily, waiting
for the onslaught of denials and the subsequent
tongue lashing. But to her surprise, the postmistress did neither.

"Wha. . . what do you mean, 'with a man'?"
stammered Miss Twickham.

The vicar was quick to take advantage of the
postmistress's obvious distress. "Just what I said,
Miss Twickham. . .and don't deny it. *You were
seen with a man.*"

"And who is making this accusation?" demanded Miss Twickham, her chin thrust out de-
fiantly.

"My sister, Amy," said the vicar smoothly.
"She saw you with a man on the pier last
night. .or rather, this morning."

As quickly as it had come, the redness left Miss
Twickham's face and she began to laugh. Un-
nerved by this unexpected change of attitude,
Richard Purdy hastened on with his explanation.
"Amy couldn't sleep, so she got up to make some
cocoa. While she was waiting for it to cool off,

she happened to glance out her bedroom window
and there you were, down on the pier with a
man. Now don't deny it.''

"Reverend Purdy, would you please tell your
sister that she is sadly mistaken,'' said the
postmistress. "I definitely was not anywhere
near the harbor last night.''

"But she saw you,'' said the vicar, wretched
that his mountain of evil thoughts should crum-
ble to the ground. "She even described you!''

"Oh, it may have been a tourist,'' intervened
Emily tentatively.

The vicar thoughtfully considered this, and
finally said slowly, clearly not liking the idea, "I
suppose it's possible, although the tourist homes
haven't opened for the season as yet.''

"Believe me, I'm not doubting your sister's
word, vicar,'' said Miss Twickham. "I'm sure she
must have seen someone who resembled me.''

"But—''

Miss Twickham held up a hand. "It was not me.
And I consider the subject closed,'' she said firmly.

All three turned as the door opened and Alicia
Rochmere came in, her shopping bag bulging.

"Ah, good afternoon, Miss Rochmere. Looks as
though you've a heavy load there,'' said the postmistress.

"Good afternoon, Miss Twickham. Not so
heavy as it is bulky, I'm afraid,'' said Miss
Rochmere, placing the bag on the floor by the
counter. With a bob of her head, she acknowledged the others. "Good afternoon, Miss King,
Reverend Purdy.''

Emily, grasping the opportunity to get the
vicar's mind off Miss Twickham, said, "The vicar

was just telling us that our little church has been robbed."

The smile left Alicia Rochmere's face, and she turned toward the vicar, "Oh, my, how terrible! Who would do such a thing?"

"I really don't know," he said. Then, glaring at Miss Twickham, "I thought we might have some help in finding the culprit, but I'm afraid I'm getting no cooperation and I have come to the unfortunate conclusion that the only thing to do is to keep the church locked at all times."

"What a shame." Alicia Rochmere's face showed genuine distress. "It seems such a pity we won't be able to go in just when we want to. After all, a house of worship should be open when a person feels the need for meditation."

"Well, I'm afraid we have no recourse, Miss Rochmere," said the vicar, "but you can always get the key at the vicarage."

"Yes," piped up Miss Twickham, "but it just isn't the same as feeling free to walk in. Many people are too shy to go to the vicarage and ask for the key."

"Well..." said the Reverend Richard Purdy, with a great sigh, "I can't think what else to do, short of having someone in there all the time."

"Perhaps when the tourist season is over?" queried Miss Rochmere.

"We'll see. However, it hasn't even begun and you see what's happened," said the vicar. He turned toward the postmistress and, like a tenacious dog with a bone, said, "Miss Twickham, are you quite sure...?"

"Quite," snapped Miss Twickham coldly.

Richard Purdy shrugged his bony shoulders. "Then I'll just go 'round and tell Sergeant Rawlins that my sister was mistaken."

"I have to be going, too," said Emily. "I've been gone too long already, and Mr. Knight will be back before I know it."

"I'll pop over in a few minutes, Miss King," said Miss Rochmere. "Mr. Knight mentioned the other day he had come across a cream jug that matched my mother's tea set. I'd like to buy it, but I'll stop at the butcher's first."

"We'll see you then," said Emily, and with those words, she made a thankful exit.

When Emily arrived back at the shop, George Knight still hadn't returned from the Hall. Putting down her purse and pastries, she shucked her coat. She felt much better now, and it was time to get some work done. The first order of the afternoon was to inspect the new delivery. There was really no reason she should hesitate about opening the crate. Mr. Knight might be spending longer than usual at the museum, for after all, there was only a week left before the opening, and she knew things were piling up. He also had to take time out to attend that estate auction this evening, and she recalled he had said something about having to go to London for a few days next week. Besides, with her experience, she was perfectly capable of inspecting and reporting on an antiquity. Getting a screwdriver from the cupboard, Emily approached the task with vigorous determination. The corner bracings of the crate were held together with glue and wire and further secured with nuts and bolts. The top of the box was held fast by sixteen screws, all deeply imbedded in the soft wood around the framework. If these were removed, the crate could be opened. Without further to-do, Emily plunged the screwdriver into the groove of a screw.

"Emily!" The screwdriver clattered to the floor at the unexpected bellow. George Knight was standing in the doorway between shop and workroom, his face almost the color of his pink shirt. "What... are... you... doing?" he asked, between clenched teeth.

"I... I was just opening the crate..." she stammered and then indignation took over. "It was delivered this morning and I thought I should open it," she said defensively.

Immediately, the little proprietor was contrite. "I'm sorry, Emily," he said, scurrying over and retrieving the screwdriver, "and I didn't mean to sound so harsh. But you took me by surprise, you see, and for insurance reasons, I always make it a point to unpack my shipment myself. You know that," he admonished lightly. He smiled at her in an attempt to make amends.

But Emily was not to be mollified so easily. "I had no intention," she said flatly, "of overstepping my duties. I simply thought it would save you time."

"And so it would, so it would," agreed her employer, "and I apologize for my outburst." He turned to look at her and smiled again, then spying the package from the bakeshop, exclaimed, "Ah! I see you've picked up my cake order." He rubbed the palms of his hands together in anticipation. "Let's gorge ourselves, shall we, and be friends again." Deftly he snapped the string and removed the cakes, fastidiously folding the white paper they had been wrapped in and placing it up on the shelf. "Waste not, want not," he said, by way of explanation. He plugged in the kettle, then came over and took Emily's arm. "Come on now, Emily," he pleaded. "I was wrong, so let's let bygones be bygones."

Emily gave him a tentative, agreeable smile, but any verbal acquiescence Emily might have made was cut off by the banging of the shop door followed by a "Hello, anybody home?" George Knight hurried out into the front of the shop, leaving Emily to tend to the tea.

"Margaret Cathcart! I might have known it would be you!" said the Bell's proprietor. "No one else I know of could make such a boisterous entrance!"

"Thank you, George," said Margaret, a hint of sarcasm in her voice, "and it's good to see you, too!"

Once again George Knight found himself apologizing. "Now, now, don't misunderstand me. I didn't mean it as an insult, really I didn't. It's, uh, just a fact," he added ineffectively.

"Well," said Margaret, her face breaking into a smile, "I don't feel insulted, so we shan't dwell on it." She stripped off her gloves. "I hope I'm not interrupting you, George? I dropped in on Amy Purdy, and since I was driving by I thought I'd stop in here and say hello."

George Knight glanced outside at the black car in front of the window. The driver's seat was empty.

"Franks isn't there, George. He's doing an errand for me."

"Well, it is nice to see you again, Margaret. You and Elizabeth arrived this morning, I take it? I saw the car driving by the coach house." The

little man eyed her appraisingly. "You're looking
your usual fit self. How's Elizabeth?"

"She's fine, thank you, George," said Margaret. "She'll be disappointed you won't be at
dinner this evening. She often says how much
she enjoys discussing antiques with you."

"Ah, yes. Charles's party. I'm sorry, too, but
I've been waiting for this particular collection to
come up for a good long while. I'll see her within
the next few days, though. Tell me, have you
seen the museum?"

"No, I haven't had the time yet."

"I think you'll be surprised at the extent of the
exhibits," said Mr. Knight, busily rearranging a
German shepherdess for the fourth time in as
many minutes. "There are some rare and unusual things."

"Yes. Charles told me about the dollhouse,"
said Margaret wryly.

"Oh, pooh!" said George, reaching for a duster.
"There's that, yes, but I think Charles overrates
it. There are other items that I think are much
more interesting."

"When I go down there, you can tell me all
about them."

"I should be delighted, Margaret, but you
needn't wait for me. Charles is almost as much of
an expert as I am."

This last was spoken with a vanity Margaret
chose to ignore. "I'm sure he is, George," she
said dryly, "and speaking of experts, Charles
mentioned you have a new assistant. A Miss
King?"

"Oh, yes, Margaret, but she's not a full-time
assistant," fussed Mr. Knight, vigorously shaking
his head. "I couldn't afford that luxury! Oh, my,

no! She's very kindly helping out while my time is taken up by your cousin's project.''

"That's what Charles explained. I understand she's a curator of a museum?'' pumped Margaret.

"In Canada," offered Mr. Knight. "And she's an assistant curator."

Margaret's eyes took in the shop area. "I was hoping she'd be here so I could meet her. I thought perhaps it would break the ice, as it were, if we met before the dinner party. Conversation, somehow, always seems so stilted when strangers are thrown together in a room full of people.''

"That's very thoughtful of you, Margaret," said the little man, flicking bits of imaginary dust off a bisque lamp. "She's in the back now." He skipped toward the back of the shop. "Just a moment. I'll get her.''

Surprisingly, even though the conversation between George Knight and Margaret Cathcart had been held only a few feet away from her, Emily hadn't heard a thing that was said, so lost was she in her own thoughts. Making tea, she'd determinedly put the brief unpleasantness with George Knight out of her mind and found herself mulling over the conversation that had taken place across the street. Really! Something should be done about the Reverend Richard Purdy! He had far too loose a tongue when it came to denouncing others! And of all the ridiculous accusations! She certainly didn't blame Miss Twickham for getting angry and denying everything. She would, too!

But it wasn't until Emily was pouring milk into her employer's cup, that she realized Miss Twickham hadn't denied everything. In fact, thought

Emily, the postmistress had only refuted the charge of being on the pier, not that she was with a man!

She was so stunned by this revelation that George Knight had to repeat her name twice before she heard. Quickly she roused herself. "Yes, Mr. Knight?"

"I'd like you to meet a dear friend of mine."

Dutifully, Emily went to the front of the shop, where a woman in a brown mackintosh immediately extended her hand, her blue eyes twinkling under the brim of an outlandish straw hat. "Miss King, I'm Margaret Cathcart. Colonel Hawkins's cousin. How very nice to meet you. I understand you'll be at our little dinner party tonight, and of course, I could have waited and been introduced then, but I always feel it's nicer to meet people before a large gathering. One simply doesn't get to know a person at all in a crowded room."

Emily, taking the proffered hand, liked Margaret instantly. "Oh, yes, Miss Cathcart, I know just what you mean about strangers meeting at a large gathering. It can be very nerve-racking."

"This evening you must tell me all about Canada. Your work sounds fascinating. I've never met a museum curator before."

"Assistant," interjected Mr. Knight.

Margaret shut him off with a blink and turned back to Emily. "And now," she cooed sweetly, "I believe there's only one other person I need to introduce myself to—your friend, Mrs. Loft."

"Sarah?" said Emily blankly, momentarily taken off guard. "Oh, I'm afraid she wouldn't be available. She writes in the afternoon and refuses to be disturbed."

"Dear me, artists can be very temperamental, can't they?" said Margaret. "I have a close friend, quite a successful painter, who couldn't blend two colors unless the 'Grand March' from *Aida* was blaring full blast. He was immune to it, of course, but it was more than a little upsetting to anyone within earshot. Finally out of sheer desperation—he had so many interruptions because of neighbors banging on his door—he moved to a secluded farmhouse!"

Emily laughed. "Thank heavens Sarah isn't like that!"

"Oh, but that's not the end of my story," continued Margaret. "In a letter I received recently, he now says one of the local farmers is complaining the cows won't give milk. I advised him to buy a boat and park himself in the middle of the English Channel, but unfortunately, he informs me he gets seasick."

Laughing, Emily shook her head in disbelief. "After hearing that story, I don't believe Sarah is at all temperamental."

"All artists are temperamental, my dear," said Margaret, suddenly serious. "I think it's because they strive for the unobtainable—perfection. Take your Mrs. Loft for instance. Most people moving to a new community are anxious to meet their neighbors and be accepted by them, but from what Miss Purdy tells me, Mrs. Loft has gone out of her way to avoid social contact. The only invitations she's accepted, in fact, have been put forth by my cousin."

"Well, she does find it difficult getting

around," explained Emily defensively, "and of course, her writing—"

"Oh, I know, my dear. Don't misunderstand me. I don't mean to criticize in any way. I'm simply trying to point out how very often artists seem independent of their surroundings. Is she writing a novel, by the way?"

"I believe so. It's in very rough stages. Frankly, at the moment, I can't make head nor tail of it," said Emily. "Come to think of it, there *is* a show of temperament. I naturally asked about her book when I arrived, but Sarah said she never discusses her work with anyone. Considers it bad luck."

"But surely as her secretary...?"

There was a loud thumping on the door, and Mr. Knight, who had retreated for his tea and cakes, scurried from the back room.

"Oh, my," exclaimed Emily, "poor Miss Rochmere."

Alicia Rochmere, her hat blown askew and her arms filled with parcels, was desperately trying to push open the door with her shoulder. Emily yanked it open, and two packages fell as the newcomer stumbled in. Margaret grabbed the little lady by the arm to help her regain her balance.

"My, oh my," said Miss Rochmere, dumping several parcels on the counter, "I swear that wind is getting stronger by the minute. It nearly blew me right off the sidewalk."

"What on earth are you doing?" asked Margaret, nodding toward the accumulation of bags and boxes. "Paying the rent for the shops in Kingscombe?"

"Oh, my dear, I don't know how I acquired so many!" wailed Miss Rochmere.

"Well, let's get them organized a bit better," said Margaret, "then I'll give you a lift home."

Swinging the door shut, Emily bent to pick up the parcels, but immediately a gust of wind blew the door open again. Annoyed, she straightened and made a move to close it once more...and then froze in horror. For suddenly she knew what had been bothering her all morning. Suddenly she knew that beyond any doubt someone—some stranger—had deliberately climbed the stairs at Rose Hill cottage last night and shut her in her room. For like the door of the shop, her bedroom door also swung inward, and the suspected draft from the hallway could only have opened it farther...not closed it!

As her shock subsided, fear of the unknown moved in. Standing on rubbery legs and leaning her head against the door, she tried to think. John! She had to see John! No sense in alarming Sarah.

"Emily!"

Fighting down the welling nausea, she forced herself back to the present surroundings.

"Emily! My goodness, child, what is your problem today?" said Mr. Knight peevishly. "Don't stand there. Shut the door!"

Automatically, Emily did as she was bidden, and picking up the parcels, she desperately tried to hide her fear. Looking up, she saw Margaret Cathcart's penetrating gaze directly on her.

"Emily," said Mr. Knight without raising his eyes from his task, "would you please fetch that string bag down from the shelf in the workroom? I think perhaps with that we could manage."

Grateful for a minute's respite, she went into the back room. Had it been imagination, or had Miss Cathcart's expression silently revealed a secret knowledge for the brief second their eyes had locked? She looked at her watch. It was surprising how a few minutes could be an eternity. In a few hours, however, John would be here and he'd know what to do. But until then, she'd have to be careful. . .but of what? She didn't know.

Returning to the front room with the string bag, she attempted to create an aura of gaiety.

"Now, Miss Rochmere, if you'll just tell me which purchases are fragile or bruisable, I'll repack them for you." To herself, her voice sounded high and unnatural, but the others appeared not to notice. For an instant, the colonel's cousin seemed about to speak and then, as though thinking better of it, clamped her mouth shut.

"Let's see, dear," said Miss Rochmere, her hand reaching for various parcels, "these are tomatoes, these are apples, these are pears, and this is fish and that is meat. Oh, and that's sewing thread and bias tape."

"What's this?" asked Emily, holding up the box with MISS A. ROCHMERE printed on it.

"That?" For a moment Miss Rochmere appeared to be at a loss. "Oh! I'm afraid I don't know."

"You don't know?" said Emily.

"No. You see. . . ." Miss Rochmere proceeded to tell about her discovery of the parcel on her doorstep.

"Why, how strange. Don't you think you'd better open it and see what it is?" asked Margaret.

"Yes, yes, I suppose I'd better," said Miss
Rochmere vaguely. "If you'll just hand it to me,
Emily, I'll open it now. That way we'll know if
it's breakable or not, won't we?" she added delightedly.

"Sit down over here," said Margaret, steering
Miss Rochmere toward the Louis XV chair and ig-
noring Mr. Knight's dance of anxiety. While Miss
Rochmere fiddled with the knot in the string,
Margaret glanced out the window and saw Miss
Twickham galloping across the street toward the
antique shop.

Margaret was sure that somewhere in a past
life Miss Twickham had been a horse. In this life,
she was tall and awkward; all arms and legs, with
a long bony face and large slightly protruding
teeth. Tight brown curls surrounding the face did
nothing to soften the illusion, and Margaret fully
expected to hear a whinny project from the wide
mouth instead of the breathless, "Oh, Miss Rochmere! I'm so glad you're still here." She produced a rumpled check from her large palm and
handed it to the frail little woman sitting in the
chair. "This check I cashed. I'm sorry, but you
didn't endorse it."

"Didn't I?" said Miss Rochmere, her eyes wide
in surprise. "How silly of me! May I borrow a
pen?" Miss Twickham fished a pen from the
deep pocket of her sweater. "Here. I have one
right here. Let me hold your parcel for you,"
she said.

Miss Rochmere smiled and handed over the
package. "Thank you, dear. We were just about
to open it." She glanced at Emily and winked.
"It's a mystery parcel!"

"A mystery parcel?" queried the puzzled post-mistress.

Miss Rochmere dismissed any further explanation with a wave of her hand. "Too long a story to go into," she said, returning the pen and check. "However, if you like, why don't you join in the fun and stay to see what it is?"

Margaret, who knew that Alicia was enjoying the attention fully, seconded the invitation, which the postmistress promptly accepted.

Miss Rochmere began to unwrap the parcel. Under the brown paper, the box was wrapped in white tissue with a plain envelope stuck to one corner. Opening the envelope, Alicia withdrew a white card, from which she read aloud:

"Roses are red, violets are blue,
Angelique comes with feeling so true,
Lean close and smell her flowers, though few,
Her little bouquet has a secret for you."

—an old friend

"How pretty!" said Emily.

"Who sent it?" asked Margaret.

"You've a secret admirer!" exclaimed Miss Twickham.

"Open it," said Mr. Knight.

Miss Rochmere's face had visibly paled. Tearing off the paper and opening the lid, she slid her hand into the layers of tissue. When she felt the cold porcelain, her face lit up in anticipation. She extracted the contents and stood up to take it over to the counter. It was a delicate piece of French porcelain—a mid-nineteenth-century music box. Standing on a pedestal was a girl, holding a bouquet of blue violets, her porcelain dress pale pink with a wide white sash. Her hair fell in dark ringlets, and on her head she wore an elaborate bonnet of pink and white porcelain lace.

"It is!" cried Miss Rochmere. "Oh, it's my Angelique!"

"She's exquisite," said Emily.

Miss Rochmere reached for the key in the bottom of the stand. Well-oiled wheels began to grind and little Angelique started to turn to the music, the hand with the flowers gently moving up and down.

All four stood enraptured, watching the little revolving figure. Miss Rochmere, lost in a world of past memories, hummed the timeless nursery tune.

"Do you know who sent it?" asked Margaret, bringing everyone back to the present.

"Hmm? Oh, yes," said Miss Rochmere, a happy little smile on her thin face and her eyes reflecting a time long gone.

"What did the card mean about smelling the flowers?" asked Miss Twickham, picking the card up off the counter. "'Lean close and smell her flowers, though few.'"

"But, of course! How silly of me to forget," said Alicia, her eyes lighting up in anticipation. Bending over the flowers, she pushed a little button hidden in the base of the nosegay. But the spring did not release the heavy sweet smell of violets as she had anticipated. Instead, the thin spray had no smell at all, but she had no time to think about that as, fire burning within her, she desperately clawed at her throat.

She was dead when she hit the floor. For a moment, the only sound to be heard in the room was Angelique's gay little nursery tune:

> Mary had a little lamb, little lamb, little
>   lamb,
> Mary had a little lamb, its fleece was white
>   as snow.
> Mary had a little. . .

. . . and then Miss Twickham began to scream and scream and scream.

5

THE MURDER ROOM had been set up at Harewood
Hall. Detective Chief Inspector Ronald Dobbs,
his stockinged feet propped up on an open desk
drawer, leaned back in the reclining swivel
chair and contemplated the cream-painted ceiling of the small paneled study off the library.
He was not a happy man. To begin with, he was
overworked, and secondly, he was unhappy because his feet hurt. This malady had started
years earlier, when he was a young constable
pounding a beat, and contrary to his hopes, it
had not been relieved when he had been pro-
moted to the luxury of a car. He had tried all
sorts of remedies, but none had given any more
than a few hours' relief. To add to his physical
discomfort, he'd been given strict orders by
his doctor to lose weight. Therefore, as a result
of his aching, burning feet and his empty
stomach, he had already been in poor humor
when the call came in from Sergeant Rawlins in
Kingscombe. At present, the only sound in the
room was the buzzing of a bumblebee, hitting
against the pane of glass, frantically seeking its
freedom.

To the other officer in the room, his tall lean
frame perched on the edge of a straight-backed
chair, the silence was becoming unbearable. He

eyed the bee sympathetically, debating whether
or not he should open the window and chance his
superior's ill humor at having his thoughts interrupted, or just let the poor thing fend for itself.
His eyes shifted from the bee to the inspector.
For years, Sergeant Buckingham's wife had been
saying that all Ronald Dobbs needed was a good
woman to take care of him, and at present the
sergeant was thinking maybe she was right. Perhaps a wife was just what the inspector needed—
someone to soothe him, smooth his rough edges
and give him less in the world to be cranky
about. He sighed audibly, and once more focused
on the bee. Fortunately, any decision he was
about to make regarding the insect was abruptly
thwarted when the big man at the desk asked,
"What do you think, Bucks?"

Detective Sergeant Buckingham took a full
minute to answer the query, considering the reply in his slow, deliberate way. He cleared his
throat. "Regarding the deceased, I really
couldn't say. But it's my opinion, sir, we've some
really queer ones in this case. Especially the...
ah...ahem...the vicar, sir."

For the first time that day, his superior allowed
himself to smile. Closing his eyes and reclining
his head against the back of his chair, he visual-
ized the day's events. "My, oh my, yes," he
mused. "The Reverend Purdy. That was quite an
education in itself, wasn't it, Sergeant?"

"I've never heard anything like it in my life,
sir."

THEY'D ARRIVED, with the lab men close on their
heels, upon a scene of mild chaos. Constable
Reed, standing at the closed door of the shop,

was attempting to keep the knots of passersby, seeking a peek at what was going on, moving off down the road. Pushing through a group of young people, the inspector and Sergeant Buckingham had made their way into the shop, where the first person to accost them was a pudgy little man wearing a pink shirt.

"Well! I do hope you'll do something about that man!" he said, pointing a pudgy finger at a red-faced Sergeant Rawlins, who was holding two pieces of what was once a bowl.

Under the inspector's penetrating stare, the sergeant felt the heat rising to his face. "It couldn't be helped, sir. One of 'em was going to touch the figurine there," he said, nodding to the music box, now carefully bagged in plastic, "and my elbow accidentally knocked this off the counter when I grabbed for her hand."

"Evidence?" inquired the inspector.

"I believe so, sir. Seems things were fine until Miss Rochmere handled it."

"No one touched anything?" asked the inspector anxiously.

"No, sir. Caught her just in the nick of time."

The inspector nodded in satisfaction. "Good lad," he said. "Where is the lady?"

"In the back, sir, along with the rest of the witnesses."

The inspector made his way toward the workroom. Placing himself in the archway, the sergeant nodded toward the three women grouped in the far corner. "Miss Twickham, sir," he said, "the one sitting down."

The inspector studied the women. Two were standing, one quite young, with wide pretty eyes, or at least they would have been, thought the inspector, if they weren't so red-rimmed and filled with fear, and the other, an older woman wearing one of the most preposterous hats the inspector had ever seen. Her arm was around the girl's shoulders and she appeared to be soothing her. Sitting to their left was a horse-faced woman, with red eyes and nose, who kept making resounding noises into a bedraggled handkerchief. "I'll speak to them in a moment," said the inspector. His eyes moved to a blond young man sitting at the rolltop desk, busily writing in a notebook. The black bag next to his elbow indicated his physician's status.

"Well, *somebody* has to pay for it!"

The inspector's attention reverted to the round little man standing behind him. "I'll see it's taken care of, Mr. . . .?"

"Knight, sir. George Knight. I own the Bell."

"I gathered as much," said the inspector. "My sergeant will take down the details." Within seconds, Sergeant Buckingham, his pad and pencil in hand, tactfully steered Mr. Knight out of earshot of the room's three other occupants.

By now, the display room had become the domain of the lab men, and the inspector led Sergeant Rawlins to the far end so that he could survey the whole scene, his narrowed eyes missing nothing and his quick mind cataloging minutiae for later sifting. "Now, Sergeant," he said, watching a photographer efficiently snap pictures of the body, "while we're waiting for the photographer to finish, fill me in on the circumstances, please."

Sergeant Rawlins opened his notebook and read the facts. "The call came in at 2:46 P.M. from Dr. Cotes. He said he had what he sus-

pected was a possible homicide to report. A Miss
Alicia Rochmere of 21 Ledbury Lane, Kingscombe, had died in the Bell Antique Shop, High
Street, under what he termed, and I quote, 'very
suspicious circumstances.' I told him to leave
everything as is and he said the door to the shop
had been locked and no one who was present at
the death of Miss Rochmere had left the
premises. When Constable Reed and myself arrived, Mr. George Knight, the owner of the Bell,
answered our knock. Inside, we found Miss Emily King, his young assistant; Dr. Cotes; Miss
Margaret Cathcart, a cousin of Colonel Hawkins
of Harewood Hall who's visiting from London;
and Miss Joyce Twickham, newsagent and postmistress from the shop just across the street. On
the floor was the body of a Miss Alicia Rochmere,
lying on her back, the right leg bent under the
body, the right hand clutching her throat, and
her left hand flung out to the side.'' The inspector looked down at the departed, who stared
sightlessly at the ceiling.

As the sergeant went on to give the witnesses'
account of what had happened, the inspector
glanced at Angelique, whose grinning porcelain
lips smiled at him in childish innocence through
the plastic. ''It has a little button,'' said the
sergeant, ''that, when pushed, emits a fine spray
from the bouquet. According to the witnesses,
Miss Rochmere pushed the button and the next
second she was falling to the floor. Dr. Cotes was
summoned by a telephone call from Mr. George
Knight and was here within ten minutes, but she
was dead when he arrived. Again, according to
witnesses, she appeared dead when she hit the
floor.''

Sergeant Rawlins snapped his notebook shut, pleased with his own thoroughness.

"Thank you, Sergeant," said the inspector, "that was an excellent report." He pushed himself off the wall. "I think I'll talk to the ladies first."

The "ladies" were much the same as he had left them, although now the horse-faced woman had composed herself. The youngest, however, was the one he was concerned with at the moment, for she still stared at the far wall as though transfixed; the continuous talking by the other woman was obviously getting no reaction. The inspector's booming voice, however, created the desired effect.

"Detective Chief Inspector Dobbs," he said, "and I believe you're Miss King, are you not?" Emily swung her eyes over to the big man. "I want you to sit down. You're looking rather peaked."

Suddenly Emily's legs felt like water, and without Margaret's support she would have fallen. "Yes. . . yes, I think I'd better. I . . . I feel rather faint."

"Perhaps the doctor should . . ." began the inspector.

"No!" The past night's incidents and Mrs. Dawson's "pill" flashed into Emily's mind. "I mean, I . . . I don't like to take medicine if I can help it. A cup of tea. . . . Perhaps that would help. There's . . . there's a hot plate next to the desk."

"I'll make you some," said Margaret, "you just sit there."

"I still think something stronger," said the inspector.

"No . . . no, tea will be fine," said Emily.

The inspector heaved a sigh. "Very well," he said. "Miss Cathcart, will you look after her, please?"

Margaret gave no indication she was surprised that he knew her name.

"Of course, Inspector. I'll settle her down a bit."

The doctor, who had been talking to Sergeant Buckingham, approached the inspector. "I wonder if I may leave now, sir. I would like to get back to my surgery. I've told your sergeant all the pertinent facts of my finding the body."

"Certainly. I know you're a busy man and I shan't keep you much longer. Just one or two questions?"

"Of course."

"You are absolutely positive it couldn't have been a heart attack?"

"Positive. Four witnesses told me that right away."

"Oh?" said the inspector. "How's that?"

"A heart-attack victim doesn't claw at his throat," said Dr. Cotes simply.

The inspector couldn't argue with logic. "Then can you hazard a guess as to what she died of?"

"Only generally. Certainly a strong dose of poison. . . and whatever it was acted instantaneously, which is unusual in itself. I'm not an authority on poisons, of course, but I do know that a person usually lives for at least a short time after exposure." Dr. Cotes shrugged resignedly. "Then again, each person is different, and Miss Rochmere was rather frail."

The inspector perked up his ears. "Oh? You were treating her?"

"No, not for anything specific. I suppose you might say her malady was loneliness. Funny, really. She lived here all her life and yet she wasn't active in village affairs. Kept to herself, developed poor habits—not eating or sleeping properly, losing weight. That's why she came to me. I couldn't find anything physically wrong with her to account for her weight loss, so I simply supplemented her diet with vitamins."

"Her heart. . ." began the inspector.

". . . was quite strong. For a person her age," qualified the doctor. "Other than that, there's really nothing more I can tell without an autopsy."

"I quite understand, doctor," said the inspector. "And I don't see why your patients should be kept waiting. I will want to see you later, however."

"Certainly, Inspector." Dr. Cotes extracted a card from his wallet. "Here's my card. I'm at your disposal."

Constable Reed approached them. "Sorry to interrupt, sir, but the Reverend Purdy is insisting on seeing Miss Rochmere. In fact, sir," he said, nervously glancing toward the front door, "he's becoming rather vehement. Says he'd like to say a few prayers over the body."

"Oh," said the inspector, "I suppose we'd better let him. But on no account," he added hastily, "is he to touch anything."

Constable Reed turned on his heel and quickly crossed the room to admit the minister.

The gray-faced man turned lightly green when he saw the contorted face of Miss Rochmere. However, squaring his shoulders, he made the sign of the cross and began to incant loudly, *"Oremus. Clementissime Deus, Pater miseri-cordiarum...."*

The others in the room went blithely about their business. Not out of disrespect, but because time was of the essence and there was no doubt in any of their minds that the deceased's last wish—had she had the time to make one—would be that her murderer be caught. They were determined to see that he, or she, was.

"...ut eius anima in hora exitus...."

"I see you've met our vicar," whispered Margaret, joining the inspector in the little archway.

Turning his head to the right, the inspector had to duck quickly to avoid the quail feather that threatened to pierce his eye. "Er, no, I haven't actually met him, Miss Cathcart," he whispered back. "Constable Reed said he wanted to pray for Miss Rochmere...but I'm surprised he's doing it in Latin. I thought that sort of thing was long gone."

"Ah, yes," said Margaret, nodding eagerly, "but no one's ever accused our vicar of being quite right in the head, Inspector. There's no telling what he'll do at any given time. As to why he feels it necessary to chant away in Latin, well, heaven only knows."

The inspector nodded, then looked back into the room behind and indicated Emily. "How is Miss King?"

"I've laced her tea with brandy. George Knight produced it from the dark recesses of a cupboard. I'd never have expected him to have such a thing. I've never seen him accept anything but tea."

"Surprising what secrets a murder reveals," murmured the inspector.

"It's just too bad," whispered Margaret, "these revelations have to be at the cost of someone's life."

Without missing a beat, the vicar raised his bowed head and glared in their direction.

"I'm afraid I'm considered a heartless heathen," hissed the inspector.

"Not at all," said the woman beside him. "I'm sure that look was meant for me."

At last the Reverend Richard Purdy ceased his litany and crossed over to the inspector and Margaret. "Thank you, Inspector, for letting me save the soul." He sighed and looked back at the body. "Evil, evil everywhere today." Turning to the inspector, he said suddenly, "Did you hear about our church, Inspector?"

"No."

"It was broken into during the night—I reported it to the police this morning—and now something like this!"

A murder hardly compared with a robbery, thought the inspector, as the vicar shook his head sadly and tut-tut-tutted, "There is so much wickedness in the world today that one cannot possibly cope with it. Mark my words, the devil is hiding everywhere, behind many innocent faces."

"I believe that has been going on for a good many years," said Margaret cynically.

"Nevertheless, it now seems to be more so," reproached Richard Purdy. Then, making no effort to conceal his dislike, he rudely turned his back to her and addressed the inspector. "Now, sir, in view of today's events, I do believe to-morrow's sermon needs some revision, and since the soul is now at rest, I should like to move on."

"By all means, Reverend, I won't keep you any longer. I shall want to talk with you later, however."

"Of course, Inspector," said the vicar, button-ing his coat. "I am usually at the vicarage. If not, then close by." Turning up his collar he took a few steps toward the door, then abruptly turned and came back again. "By the way, In-spector. Miss Rochmere left a will, you know. It's in the desk at the rectory. I'm the sole beneficiary, you see," he said and, without a backward look, strode outside to buck the cold wind.

Frowning, the inspector stared at the closed door.

Margaret was the first to speak. "Well, if that isn't a bombshell!"

The inspector turned his attention back to the woman standing next to him. "Yes, it is. I won-der how much she had to leave?"

"Oh, not much, I'm sure. Poor Alicia. She always seemed to be on the outside looking in. Timid. That was her problem. Afraid of the world. She never earned any money that I know of. Her father was the vicar here for years and she always looked after him. When he retired they moved to her present address. There were only the two of them. Her mother passed away years before, and I believe she had a brother—a year or so older or younger, I'm not sure—who was killed in the last war."

"For a visitor from London, you seem to

know a lot about the deceased,'' said the inspector.

Margaret shrugged. ''It's not surprising. All my school holidays were spent at Harewood—except during the war, of course, when our school was evacuated to Monmouthshire.''

''Then perhaps, Miss Cathcart, you could provide me with a list of friends of the deceased?'' Deftly avoiding the quail feather, he steered her into the back room with the others and pulled the heavy draperies, blocking out the macabre scene.

''I can do even better than that. If you're familiar with village life, Inspector, you'll know it comes in tightly knit groups, and the people who knew Alicia Rochmere will all be at my cousin's for dinner tonight. It was supposed to be a pre-opening celebration for Colonel Hawkins's latest hobby—a museum of Victorian toys—and to tell you the truth, I'd been about to ring him up asking him to call it off, in view of what's happened, but we may be doing a disservice to poor Alicia. Heaven knows it will be far from a happy occasion, but I do think it better if things are left as they are; in fact, I'll ask Charles to get in touch with the guests to make sure they know they're still expected. That way, you'll have them all together and can question them.''

''Excellent!''

''I shall also take the liberty of offering you and your men the hospitality of my cousin's home. It would be an ideal place for your headquarters. You would have complete privacy and still be close to the village and the actual murder scene.''

The inspector's respect for the brain at work under the preposterous hat had risen considerably. "My dear lady," he said, "I can't thank you enough, and with your cousin's approval of the plan, I shall be delighted to accept your invitation. Just one question. Will all the witnesses to the murder be at the dinner tonight?"

Margaret shook her head. "George Knight won't be. He was invited, but he's going to an estate auction, and Miss Twickham didn't have an invitation, but that can be remedied right now," she said, moving toward the postmistress.

She returned a few minutes later with her arm linked through Miss Twickham's. "She says she has to catch a train later this evening. She's going to a wedding and will be back Tuesday night. Do you think she could leave in time?"

"Of course," said the inspector.

"Good. Franks can drive her to the station, so there's no problem there. She also asked me to apologize for her attempt to touch the figurine. She says, and I believe her, it was purely a matter of reflex and lack of thought."

"I shall need your signed statement to that effect this evening, Miss Twickham."

"Certainly, and you shall have it," said Margaret.

The inspector was beginning to wonder if the postmistress had a voice of her own, and his first thought that Margaret Cathcart might be a help in the investigation was being superseded by grave doubts. It was now quite obvious she was a woman who liked to take over, and he was most certainly not about to have some meddling female under his feet. Well, he'd put her in her place right now.

"If you ladies will excuse me?" said the inspector, in a voice more frigid than he had intended. "Sergeant Buckingham will take preliminary statements from you, then you are free to go." With an abrupt nod to Miss Twickham, he turned on his heel and marched into the front room, snapping closed the draperies behind him.

"Now what do you suppose brought that on?" said Margaret in all innocence.

After Sergeant Buckingham had taken first-hand accounts, and informed the witnesses there would be further questions that evening, those who had viewed the crime were only too pleased to leave.

Constable Reed and Sergeant Rawlins, meanwhile, had been sent to Miss Rochmere's house to conduct a thorough search and interrogate the neighboring families. It was well into the afternoon before the lab men completed their routine tasks, and Alicia Rochmere's remains, along with little Angelique, were taken off for analysis to the forensic laboratory.

"Let's take a quick drive to the lady's home and see what our two accomplices have come up with," said the inspector when he and Buckingham emerged from the antique shop.

Constable Reed met them at the door and led them through the house. Mounting the narrow, steep staircase, he filled them in on the interviews with the neighbors. "Only two other houses in the lane, sir, and they aren't any too close. A Mr. and Mrs. Lemly live in one, with their three children. They were all home. Mr.

Lemly and the two youngest children are in bed
with the flu, and the boy, William—he's seven-
teen and a surly lad—informed us he was 'between jobs,' although it's my opinion, sir, that he
never leaves the house to look for one; we've
seen his face more than once at the station.
Nothing major, you understand. Just petty things
that warrant a good talking to—not that it seems
to have done any good in his case. At any rate,
both Mrs. Lemly and William say they saw
nothing unusual, and the other three are too sick
to even want to look out the window. Mr.
Jenkins, the postman, is the only person Mrs.
Lemly spoke to this morning, when he delivered
the mail about nine.

"Now, the other house is occupied by a young
couple who are away on holiday. Italy, according
to Mrs. Lemly. Been gone two weeks and expected back next weekend.

"Oh, and I think I should mention, sir, that
there's a public footpath that runs about one
hundred yards beyond the side of this house. It
leads directly to the village, and also can't be
seen from either of the two other houses."

"Naturally," grumbled the inspector.

There were three doors off the small landing on
which they stood. "Well, let's see where this
leads," said Inspector Dobbs, throwing open one
of them. They were confronted with a neat,
almost clinical bedroom with a meticulously
made-up bed, a polished dressing table and a
small wardrobe, which revealed three dresses,
two skirts, four blouses, two pairs of shoes, two
cardigans, and three hats. The tiny drawers of
the dressing table possessed nothing more than
serviceable underwear, gloves, stockings, and a

string of cheap pearls, along with several scarves and handkerchiefs.

The second room was small and square. It contained a cot, stripped to the mattress, and a long chest of drawers. The top drawer was filled with towels and wash cloths, the middle two were empty, and the bottom one held two blankets reeking of mothballs.

The third door led them into a compact bathroom with no personal effects other than a toothbrush, a tube of toothpaste and a hairbrush.

"A woman of few frills, our Miss Rochmere," said the inspector, as they made their way to the ground floor.

Downstairs, running along one wall in the galleylike kitchen, was a green countertop, broken only by a sink and three-burner stove. Underneath was a small refrigerator, as well as cupboards containing tins of food and pots and pans. A cupboard above the sink revealed a few dishes, and the single drawer held cutlery and two tea towels. A table and two chairs were pushed against the other wall.

Lastly, there was the living room, where an overstuffed sofa and chair, their wine-colored plush covers protected by ecru lace antimacassars, dominated the space. The tiled mantelpiece and the tops of a color television set and two small tables were heavily burdened with vividly colored, miniature glass animals.

"Well, this certianly makes up for the few frills upstairs! The only thing missing from this place is a tabby," mused the inspector, standing in the doorway. As if on cue, a large cat, not a tabby but midnight black, slunk from behind the sofa and swiftly and silently leaped up onto the arm of the chair, its yellow green eyes surveying the intruders with utter disdain.

Both Inspector Dobbs and Sergeant Buckingham gave an involuntary jump.

"Sometimes I think those damn things have ESP," said the inspector, recovering from his initial shock.

Sergeant Rawlins, diligently sorting through papers stuffed in a small secretary, jubilantly held up an envelope.

"I've found a niece's address, sir," he said, handing it to the inspector. "She lives in Edinburgh."

"Good. Get on this right away, will you, Constable?" said the inspector.

"Yes, sir," said Reed. "By the way, we haven't checked the grounds yet so if you don't mind, sir, I'll go out the back door to the garden on my way."

"Good idea, Constable," said the inspector, then turning to the man at the desk, he asked, "Anything else, Sergeant?"

"No, sir. Mostly receipts, even to old grocery bills— Oh, ho! Wait a minute," he said, his fingers pulling at something stuck between the shelf and the cabinet backing. "Here's something. Looks like a bankbook. Yes, it is," he said, opening it up. "A London branch, sir."

Taking the proffered prize, the inspector flipped it open to read the final balance. A low appreciative whistle escaped his lips. "Twenty-three thousand, four hundred pounds! Now where would one sweet little lady acquire that much?" he asked.

Both sergeants peered over his shoulder as he

slowly turned the pages toward the beginning of the book.

"A picture beginning to form, Bucks?"

Sergeant Buckingham nodded solemnly. From the steady flow of unwavering monthly deposit amounts, a picture was indeed beginning to form. "Blackmail, sir. Pure and simple. Our sweet little lady was blackmailing someone!"

The back door banged open, and Constable Reed, vainly trying to keep the excitement out of his voice, barged in from the kitchen, sidestepped the cat and slid to a stop in the doorway.

"Sir," he gasped, "there's something very odd out here. I should have looked sooner." He hurriedly turned and retraced his steps, all three men clambering after him and stopping just inside the door to let the inspector pass through first. He took three steps and stopped in his tracks.

"Good God! Who would have done it?"

It had been a garden of flowers. A great abundance of flowers: wallflowers, tulips, lilacs, primulas, four o'clocks—a garden to take pride in. But now no artist's mass of color met the eye. In fact, the whole area was a disaster. There were no leaves and blooms on the plants—only stark, spindly stalks of green and brown shooting up forlornly from the rich earth. All the bright flowers and lush foliage that would have delighted the eye lay in a wilting heap against the back of the walled garden, where they obviously had been thrown not too many hours before.

THE TELEPHONE RANG in the small study, bringing
both men back to the present. While his superior
talked, Sergeant Buckingham took the opportunity to open the window and release the bee.
The call was from Sergeant Rawlins, saying that
Mr. Jenkins had seen nothing untoward when
he'd delivered the mail that morning, although
he'd had none for Miss Rochmere. Also, they'd
found four more savings books, each one taped
between the drawers and the desk backing. The
monthly deposits of one hundred pounds covered
a period of nineteen and a half years—from the
winter of 1942 to the summer of 1961. Replacing
the receiver, Inspector Dobbs related the conversation to his sergeant.

"Why did it stop then?" asked the inspector, as
much to himself as anyone.

"Maybe her quarry died," offered Sergeant
Buckingham.

"That's the logical explanation," agreed his
superior, "and yet, when a blackmailer is murdered, you can't help but surmise it's done by the
victim."

"Maybe there are more bankbooks somewhere?" suggested the sergeant.

The inspector shook his head. "We've covered
every nook and cranny in that house, Bucks.
There were no other bankbooks." He pursed his
lips together in thought. "Nineteen forty-
two. . . . Let's check out who of this bunch was in
Kingscombe that year. Something must have
gone on?. . . And then there's that damn figurine.
Each of the witnesses swears Miss Rochmere said
she knew who sent it."

"Perhaps after the lab has gone over it. . . ." offered the sergeant.

"I doubt it." Exasperated, the inspector ran his hand through his iron-gray hair. "Somehow I have a feeling this one's going to be a stinker. And the back garden...! What was the point of that?" He sighed. "I can't figure out how anyone could have got in, either, except through the house, and the front door and windows were always kept locked. You saw the garden, eh, Bucks? Enclosed on one side by the house, and on the other three sides by an eight-foot wall with shards of glass embedded along the top. Impossible to climb over it."

"But there is a gate...." began the sergeant.

"Yes, but it's only a little lower than the wall, and it, too, had those shards of glass. Furthermore, it opens by a latch on the inside. I see no way it can be opened from the street."

"But the wall was scaled somehow. After all, there was that print, sir."

Sergeant Rawlins was referring to a perfect plimsoll footprint they'd found in the soft garden earth. They'd protected it with a board and called the lab men to make a plaster cast. The print was obviously too large for Alicia, and besides, she didn't even own a pair of plimsolls.

"Yes," said the inspector, his face brightening a little. "But how could someone have scaled that damn wall? I noticed there were no juttings for handholds, nothing for a rope to loop over...."

"What about that tree? The branches grow over the storage-shed roof."

"None of those branches could hold any weight," replied his superior.

"A ladder, then, sir?"

"I can't see it, Bucks. Even with an accomplice

to remove the ladder, there's still the chance of someone seeing him, and where the devil is he going to put it, anyway, other than in a van? No, it's too much of a long shot. It would take too long to do, and secondly, I can't see anyone taking a chance leaning over that jagged glass. One slip, and he could be done for, if an artery were pierced.''

''I see what you mean,'' said the sergeant, ''but it's a damned aggravating puzzle. Do you think it was done by the murderer?''

''I don't know, Bucks, I don't know.''

An ominous rumbling came from the inspector's stomach. Sergeant Buckingham squirmed in his chair and looked at his watch. All week it had been like this, about half an hour before mealtime.

''What time is it, Bucks?''

''Six thirty-eight, sir. Only twenty-two minutes more. I've asked for a tray to be sent in at seven.''

''And what succulent repast do we have tonight?'' drawled his superior.

The sergeant cleared his throat. It was difficult to tell a gourmet cook whose culinary taste ran to *cordon bleu* fare with rich sauces, that he was to dine on lean meat, sliced tomatoes, green beans and jelly, and just as he thought, the inspector did not receive the news graciously.

''Damn it all, Buckingham!'' he said, emphasizing his feelings by slamming a palm onto the polished desk. ''That doctor had no business putting me on a diet!''

''No, sir. I agree,'' said the sergeant, with more temerity than he felt, but hoping against hope that knowing he had someone in his corner would improve the inspector's mood. "Nevertheless, we should stick to it, sir; the less you eat, the sooner you'll lose the weight. And really, sir, the meal doesn't sound too bad," he added feebly.

"You don't have to eat it," said his superior irritably. Abruptly he reined in his irrationality and sighed. "Bucks, how do you put up with me?"

"I suppose it's easy because we've been a team so long, sir, and we've grown used to each other. And I wouldn't say you're always difficult to get along with," he added hastily, although at the moment, the sergeant was hard put to think of a time when the inspector had been easy to please.

The big man threw back his head and guffawed. "You're a good friend, Sergeant, and also a pretty good liar. I know how miserable I've been this past week, and when I get off this blasted fasting, I'm taking you and the missus out for an eight-course dinner!" He patted his paunch. "And now that my stomach has been somewhat appeased by the thought of food, meager fare though it is, I think we should get down to work." Uprighting the chair, he hunched over the desk. "Let's go over that list of tonight's guests. I want to have their connection with the deceased straight in my mind. First, those we haven't met."

"There are four, sir," said Sergeant Buckingham, looking at a slip of paper he pulled from his pocket. "Mrs. Marion Bundy, Miss Amy Purdy, Mrs. Sarah Loft and Mr. John Trask."

"Good, good. Let's start with Mrs. Bundy."

MARION BUNDY WAS ANNOYED with herself. That
stupid near-accident this morning...and with
Charles's car, of all cars! By rights, she should
have called him and apologized, but she'd been
running late, her mind on other things; and since
no harm had been done, she decided to go to the
horse sale in Exeter and wait until the evening to
apologize in person. But when she'd returned
home, that silly girl, Grace, had met her at the
door, babbling about Alicia Rochmere dropping
dead in the Bell. She couldn't get any more out of
her other than that the police had been called in,
and that Colonel Hawkins had phoned to say he
was still having the dinner party, which seemed
in rather bad taste, thought Marion, considering
one of the guests had recently met her demise.
Grace also told her that Margaret Cathcart had
telephoned.

Sending Grace up to run her bath, Marion had
tried several times to telephone Charles Hawkins
to voice her opinion on his continuing with the
party, but each time she received a busy signal.
Finally, she had called up Richard Purdy to see
what was what, but all she could get out of him
was a dissertation on the evils of the soul. Utterly
exasperated, she'd banged down the receiver
and gone upstairs to her bedroom to gather her
thoughts.

Marion had no illusions about herself. Of the
men she came into contact with, none of them
desired her as a woman. To come out on top in a
highly competitive business, one had to be ruthless and calculating. She thought like a man and
fought like one.

Only in the seclusion of her own rooms did she
let the barriers down. Thus, her bedroom re-

flected a Marion none of her acquaintances ever suspected existed, and as soon as she closed the door, she felt better. It was a room with laces and satins, and mirrored walls that reflected its occupant in multifaceted images. Her vanity table was covered with expensive creams and lotions. The dressing room contained several exercise machines and the adjoining bathroom looked as though it belonged in a cosmetic salon. The floor was broadloomed in three-inch-thick white fur carpet. One entire wall was covered with bottles of astringents, oils, salts, jars of talcs and boxes of dusting powder, and indirect lighting in a soft pink glow played with jewel-like fingers on the array of colored glass bottles. Mammoth bath towels were stacked on the counter top to one side of the sink, and the sunken tub was black and gold marble, surrounded on three sides by luscious tropical plants. When Marion submerged into the clinging oils of the just-so-hot bath water, she insisted the room be filled with steam. Thus Grace would, while pouring the bath, run the hot-water tap in the sink and spray perfume.

So now, when Marion Bundy stepped from her pink-and-white dressing room into her bathroom, she entered a new world, a subtropical paradise heavily scented with jasmine.

It took twenty-five minutes for the temperature of the bath water to fall below the point Marion found pleasant. This was her cue to continue to the next phase of her bathing ritual, and emerging from the tub, she reached for the heavily woven bath towel...and immediately spotted the discordant note in the symphony of bottles. There, on the fifth shelf, at eye level and standing in front of the bottle of rosewater and the milk-glass jar filled with blue hyacinth dusting powder, was a pink glass bottle she had never seen before. A pink satin ribbon around the neck held a white card in place.

Frowning, Marion reached out for the bottle and turned the card over. There, neatly type-written, were the words:

> Jonquils are yellow, pansies are, too,
> An old friend sends this gift to you,
> Yesterdays we had so sweet
> Until tonight... when again we'll meet!

Perplexity furrowing her brow, Marion stood, with the towel draped around her, holding the bottle. She removed the lid and held the bottle to her nostrils. Suddenly her eyes lit up and a smile of happiness spread across her face.

The scent was Ashes of Roses. It had to be him! She hadn't forgotten, Marion thought, so why should he? Slowly she read the card again and the last line put her into sheer ecstasy. "Until tonight...." Where? When? The party? No—she shook her head—that would have been too ob-vious. But then...? "Oh dear God," prayed Marion, "Let it go right this time."

With trembling hands, she smoothed the lotion liberally over her skin. As the old, familiar, haunting scent permeated the air, nebulous thoughts filtered in and out of her mind. Where was he now? What had he been doing all these years? Would she live up to his expectations? She was literally shaking with nervousness and ex-citement. With concentrated effort, she forced herself to relax. "Get hold of yourself, Marion," she said aloud, "or you'll never make it through this evening."

Forty-five minutes and several glasses of sherry later, the new Marion, dressed in billowing pink tulle, auburn hair piled high on her head, walked sedately down the stairs to the waiting vehicle. Grace, watching her walk across the hall, thought she had never seen Mrs. Bundy look so beautiful.

By the time the car pulled up in front of the lighted steps of Harewood Hall, the alcohol had done its work, and the mistress of Redwing felt composed and self-assured. How glad she was that she hadn't been able to contact Charles to cancel the party!

6

DESCENDING THE STAIRS dressed in her new
mauve crepe gown, a shade totally at odds with
her coloring, Margaret could hear a babel of
voices coming from beyond the drawing-room
doors. Instead of turning right to join the guests,
she crossed the hall toward the library. At present, she did not feel up to discussing the day's
events with anyone, a thought she found surprising, for she prided herself on being able to meet
and deal with a crisis head-on . . . but then again,
she'd never come upon a murder before. Yes,
definitely a stimulating glass of good rich port
was called for to soothe her jangled nerves. This
afternoon had not been easy. Easing her way
through the partially opened library door, she
felt her feet sink into the deep pile of moss-green
carpet.

The large, book-lined room was her favorite. A
room for meditation and introspection, it smelled
of old wood, furniture polish and leather. Two
lamps, one at either end of the table in front of
the sofa, threw a soft, warm glow into the main
area of the room, leaving the outer perimeter in
deep shadow.

Margaret crossed the deep carpeting to the re-
cessed liquor cabinet at the right of the fireplace
and reached up for a glass.

Swish. She froze. The noise had come from behind and to her left. For what seemed like an eternity, she stood stock still, barely breathing, her heart pounding, as the soft brushing sound continued. Finally, realizing she was not about to be attacked, life slowly returned to her benumbed muscles, and slowly she turned toward the room. The mystery was solved instantaneously. Extending from beyond a wing chair half-hidden in the shadows was the lower half of a woman's leg, the foot encased in a silver slipper. Light glinted off bejeweled fingers twisting and straightening a stocking. Margaret cleared her throat. "Excuse me."

Hastily, lavender taffeta and chiffon was dropped over the limb.

Margaret approached the chair. "You gave me quite a start. I didn't know anyone was in here."

"No more than you gave me," said the woman. "You see, I didn't know anyone was here, either!"

The size of the chair's occupant astounded Margaret. "Are you all right?" she asked concernedly. "I mean, being in here alone. . . ."

The woman smiled. "I'm fine, thank you." She indicated her foot now hidden by the long gown. "Simply a twisted stocking."

Margaret gave a nod of understanding. For several seconds the two women sized each other up, neither one underestimating the other.

Margaret was the first to break the scrutiny. With a smile she thrust out her hand. "I'm Margaret Cathcart, Charles Hawkins's cousin, and I suspect you're Sarah Loft."

The other woman returned the smile, as glittering fingers barely touched Margaret's hand.

"Margaret Cathcart! I've been anxious to meet you. Emily told me it was you in particular who helped her get through that dreadful ordeal today. I'm very grateful."

"Don't mention it," said Margaret, going back to the cabinet. "Will you join me in a glass of port?"

"I'd like that."

Margaret picked up the thread of conversation. "I only did what anyone else would have done in similar circumstances," she insisted. "The poor child was in shock, which is understandable. Death by poison is not a pretty sight." Margaret gave an instinctive shiver as she thought of Alicia Rochmere lying on the floor of the Bell.

"I'm sure it isn't."

"Alicia was such a sweet little thing," Margaret continued, handing Sarah a glass, then sitting on a nearby chair. "I can't imagine why anyone would want to kill her. I can tell you, it will take me a long time to get over it. As a matter of fact, that's why I came in here—for fortification." She raised her glass in mock salute. "I didn't feel I could face the questions I'm sure everyone'll be asking."

Sarah, about to take a sip of her drink, raised her eyes and looked at Margaret over the rim of her glass. "You may be pleasantly surprised. I think you'll find the others avoiding any reference to Miss Rochmere's death in the same way they'd avoid a plague. When I left them, everyone was trying hard to put on a happy front and ignore what happened."

"Ugh!" said Margaret, making a face. "That attitude is more nauseating than facing the facts."

"Nevertheless, I suppose it's only natural for

the mind to shut out unpleasantness," said Sarah. "It's terrible that such a thing had to happen on your first day here."

Margaret shrugged. "Yes. . . but the odd thing is I didn't feel nearly so bad until I was subjected to one of Richard Purdy's dreadful glares at the scene of the crime. He has a horrible knack of making innocent people feel guilty, you know. I'm sure he's decided that the Devil has possessed me and that I'm to blame for the whole thing."

"Nonsense!" said Sarah. "He's known you too many years to even entertain such thoughts."

"Never underestimate the evil mind of our vicar," said Margaret advisedly. "It works in mysterious ways."

Sarah made no comment. For several moments, both women sipped their wine in silence, each in her own thoughts.

"Mrs. Loft," said Margaret softly, smoothly. An electrical current charged the room.

The other woman looked up. "Yes?"

"How did you know that Richard Purdy has known me for a long time?"

A smile tipped the corners of Sarah's lips. She always admired a keen mind. "My goodness, Miss Cathcart," she said, "you certainly sound more like an adversary than a friend! Now what would you say if I also told you that: A, you and your sister are comfortably well off; B, that your sister raised you after your mother died; C, that your father was an invalid for years, due to a riding accident; and D, that you are considered among family and friends as the bane of your sister's and cousin's peace of mind?"

Margaret was not amused. "All I can say," she

said, "for starters anyway, is that Charles has been talking out of turn."

To her annoyance, the huge woman laughed. "You're quite on the wrong track, my dear. Colonel Hawkins has never discussed his family with me. Oh, no, Miss Cathcart, call it fortune or misfortune, but in a village of this size and with Mrs. Dawson as housekeeper, gossip knows no bounds!" Smiling, she picked up her cane and added, "And now that that is cleared up, don't you think we should join the others? They'll no doubt be wondering where we are." She began to maneuver her bulk out of the chair.

"Dawson...Dawson.... That name rings a bell," said Margaret, getting up and placing the glasses on an end table. "Isn't there a Dawson at Redwing?"

"Yes," agreed Sarah. "There's Mrs. Dawson's nephew, Ben, and his sister, Grace, is a maid there."

"I've seen them, but I've never talked with them," said Margaret.

Sarah grunted herself up to a standing position. "Well, believe me, if they're as garrulous as their aunt, no one need step a foot out of the house to know what's going on in the village."

Making their way across the hall, Sarah leaning heavily on her cane, Margaret decided to ask a question that had been bothering her all day. "Mrs. Loft...Sarah, Charles mentioned this morning that you're a writer. I was wondering...what type of books do you write?"

Sarah didn't so much as break the rhythm of her shuffle. "I never discuss my writing," she said flatly, "with anyone." Her tone left no doubt that the subject was closed.

Margaret shrugged. Well, so much for that. She knew a brick wall when she ran into one, but she did make a mental note to cultivate Mrs. Dawson's friendship.

As they entered the drawing room, all the guests but one were clustered around an object at the far end of the room. The sole exception was the vicar, who was seated on one of the sofas against the wall, gloomily staring into his half-filled wine glass. It was quite obvious to the two women that their absence had caused no concern, for their entrance was noticed only by Emily and her escort, who extricated themselves from the group and came to meet them.

Not even the day's ordeal could mar Emily's happiness. John was there and all was well. No sooner had he entered Rose Hill early that evening than she'd taken him by the hand and led him out to the garden seat where she'd poured out her day. Somehow, in his presence, things had seemed lighter. He'd listened in silence while she spent her emotions and tenderly consoled her when she cried on his shoulder for poor Miss Rochmere. Only when she spoke of her nightmare and Mrs. Dawson's implication, did he take any aggressive action; and then it was to question her gently, but thoroughly. When he found her answers unsatisfactory, a hard, determined look came to his eyes—a look Emily, in her distraction, failed to see. But it lasted only a moment, and when she did look into his eyes, she saw only what she wanted to see—love and tenderness. Tonight, only the paleness of her cheeks gave any indication of the ordeal she had been through.

Sarah introduced her nephew to Margaret.

"What's going on over there?" inquired Margaret, indicating the group of guests.

"Colonel Hawkins had the dollhouse brought up from the museum," said Emily. "Have you seen it yet?"

"No, I haven't." Then, turning to Sarah, asked, "Shall we join them?"

The four made their way toward the others, walking slowly for Sarah's benefit. Maggie, the maid, approached them with a tray holding several glasses of sherry. Each took one, but they hadn't taken more than a few steps before Marion Bundy, her face unnaturally flushed, took Margaret by the elbow and rudely led her away from her companions to the opposite side of the room.

"Margaret! Where have you been hiding yourself? I knew you were here, but I didn't see you when I came in."

"I'm sorry, Marion. I was late coming down." She couldn't remember seeing the mistress of Redwing so radiant—nor so obviously a little tipsy. There was no doubt that Marion Bundy had had a few drinks other than the standard two Charles served his guests before dinner.

". . . and I must apologize for this morning! It was absolutely unforgivable! Never, never, have I done anything like it before! You will forgive me, won't you, Margaret?" Marion pouted red lips. "Charles and Elizabeth have!"

Although potentially dangerous, the morning's riding incident now seemed trivial and unimportant in view of subsequent events, and Margaret simply acquiesced. "It really doesn't matter, Marion," she said flatly. "In view of what I've been through this afternoon—"

"That's what I wanted to talk to you about! Now you must tell me all about Alicia's death," said Marion in a conspiratorial whisper that could be heard three feet away. "I couldn't get a thing out of that cousin of yours, except to learn that you were actually there! How thrilling!"

"Marion!" said the only other person within earshot. "Have you no respect for the dead?"

"Oh, nonsense," said Marion petulantly, tossing her head of auburn curls. "I say what I please, Reverend, and I can't see how you can think it sinful. After all, we all have to die some time." With a disdainful flick of a well-rounded shoulder, Marion dismissed Richard Purdy. "You know, Margaret, a thought's just occurred to me. Think of how many of us die every day. We're buried, and then are fortunate if our name is even mentioned after a few months. But one thing you have to say for Alicia is that she knew how to make an exit. Why, she'll be talked about for years. Oh, but I do think her death is thrilling, and as far as I can see, her only claim to anything was leaving this world so dramatically!"

But the vicar was not about to be put off with a flip of a shoulder. "You are an evil woman. Mark my words, God overcomes the Devil every time. You'll rue your words tonight, Marion Bundy!"

For once, Margaret was inclined to agree with Richard Purdy. There *was* something evil about Marion tonight, and with a start, Margaret realized what it was. Marion Bundy actually seemed glad that Alicia Rochmere was dead!

Glancing at the others, Margaret was gratified to see that the dollhouse still held their attention, and no one seemed aware of the verbal battle taking place between the vicar and Marion.

"Marion, I think..." Margaret began. But her
words were overridden.

"Dickie, Dickie, Dickie," taunted Marion, deliberately using the name she knew he detested.
"You're sick. All you can see is the Devil lurking
everywhere but in yourself. I think you'd be surprised at how much of dear old Beelzebub there
is in you!"

It was the last straw! Richard Purdy, his hands
clenched and knuckles white, turned on his heel
and strode across to the group gathered around
the dollhouse.

"He's crazy," said Marion coldly. "They
should lock him up."

At any other time, Margaret would have been
tempted to agree with her, but tonight she felt
oddly sorry for Richard Purdy. "Now, tell me
about Alicia's death," Marion said, with an
eagerness that Margaret found repellent.

"Marion, I don't want to talk about Alicia now.
I want to see the dollhouse, remember?"

"And so you shall," said Marion magnanimous-
ly. "But first I need a drink."

"Do you think you should?" asked Margaret.

"Now don't you start on me," said Marion.
Clinging to Margaret's arm, she steered them to
the sideboard where one full glass still sat on
Maggie's tray. "I know exactly what I'm doing.
Besides, I have a special reason to celebrate!"

Margaret made no comment. This lack of interest was not what Marion had expected, and cock-
ing her head to one side, she said teasingly,
"Wouldn't you like to know what my secret is,
Margaret?"

For the second time that evening, Margaret
reassessed her ideas. She had no idea that Marion

could be so coy. And for the first time, she saw her as a very vulnerable woman. In Marion's mood, there was no use saying no. "Only if you wish to tell me, Marion."

"You're quite right," said Marion, sipping her drink, "only if I wish to tell you." She pointed a painted finger at Margaret's left breast. "And since you're so nice, I'm going to tell you." Unceremoniously pulling Margaret toward her, she whispered, "I'm expecting to meet someone later. An old love." She pulled away. "Yes, a very dear and old love," she said, searching the fathoms of her glass. For a moment she stood there, lost in her thoughts, the swaying of her body perceptible. Then abruptly, Marion brought herself back to the present, and with a transformation Margaret found hard to keep up with, she was once again the coolheaded businesswoman. "Now, let's see my dollhouse," she said. The two women mingled with the others around the museum piece.

"It *is* lovely," said Margaret, admiring the delicate intricacies of the toy. "How did you ever acquire it, Marion?"

But Marion was in no condition to answer. Dropping her glass to the floor, she hugged her abdomen, as her eyes, wide with fear, pleaded silently for help. Before Margaret could move, she fell to the floor, writhing in pain and gasping for air. Margaret's involuntary cry immediately brought Dr. Cotes rushing over. He knelt by the stricken woman and began administering first aid, at the same time calling for someone to call for an ambulance. While Margaret rushed to the phone and the doctor attended to the convulsed woman, others posed themselves in an immobi-

lized semicircle, feeling helpless but each filled
with the repulsive, inexplicable fascination
people have when they witness another's misfortune. Emily, standing rigidly off to one side, was
the only one to hear Sarah mutter to herself,
"But she *can't* be involved!" Emily threw Sarah
a brief inquiring glance, but, when there was no
reaction, quickly forgot the comment and, like
everyone else, turned her full attention to Marion Bundy.

The door to the "murder room" flew open and
Margaret Cathcart burst in. "I think you'd better
come," she said to the two startled faces that
looked up at her. "Something's just happened to
Marion Bundy and I've rung for an ambulance."

"The devil you say!" Inspector Dobbs was out
of his seat and through the door in two seconds
flat, with Sergeant Buckingham close on his
heels. The scene they came upon was the same as
when Margaret had run out, except that now
Mrs. Bundy was no longer twisting and writhing.
Now she lay quite still.

"Is she dead?" asked the inspector harshly.

"No. In a deep coma, and her breathing's very
shallow."

The inspector knelt by Marion. "What happened?"

"I don't know," said the doctor, getting up
from his knees and dusting off his pant legs.
"I've done all I can for her here. The only thing I
will say is that it looks like another case of poisoning."

"But I was talking with her!" said Margaret.
"She was standing right behind me, drinking
sherry."

At the mention of sherry, the inspector's eyes

fell to a glass that had rolled under a small table. Unfolding a handkerchief, he picked it up between thumb and forefinger. "Would this have been hers?"

"It's logical to assume so," said Margaret. "She was standing about where you are now."

Taking Sergeant Buckingham aside, he handed him the glass. "Get it right to the lab boys, will you, Bucks? And I want all the opened bottles sent along. God knows what's been doped up. And while you're at it, find out what's taking Striker so long with that other lab report."

"Yes, sir."

A slight commotion in the hall preceded the entrance of Miss Hawsberry, followed by two ambulance attendants who, efficiently and unemotionally, transported Marion Bundy onto their stretcher.

"I'm going to the hospital with them," said Dr. Cotes, shrugging into the coat the colonel held for him. "I'll be in touch as soon as I know something definite."

"Sergeant Rawlins will meet you there," said the inspector. "If it's what you say it is, I want a twenty-four-hour guard on her room."

"Here, ring this number," said the colonel, hastily scribbling on a paper napkin. "It's a private line, direct to the study."

"It shouldn't be too long before you hear from me, Inspector," said Fred Cotes, as he climbed into the back of the ambulance. The inspector just had time for a curt nod of approval, before the attendant slammed the door shut and ran around to the cab as the motor was gunned into life.

Inspector Dobbs stood on the gravel driveway

and listened to the wail of the siren as it faded
into the distance. When the sound of chirping
crickets was all that broke the night silence, he
flexed his powerful shoulders and reentered the
house.

Standing in the doorway, he noted that a tangible pall had set in. The guests had dispersed into
small groups, whispering among themselves. The
inspector observed each knot of people individu-
ally. Richard Purdy, his sister and Joyce Twickham were near the dollhouse, both ladies quietly
crying into handkerchiefs. Midway along the
room, Emily King and Elizabeth Cathcart were
talking with a very fat woman and a handsome
young man, whom the inspector assumed to be
Sarah Loft and her nephew. Margaret Cathcart
was not anywhere to be seen. Only the colonel
was alone, sitting in a large armchair, head
bowed. Inspector Dobbs approached him.

"Colonel Hawkins. I'd like to question your
guests now. Privately."

"Eh?" The colonel looked up, uncomprehend-
ing.

"I said, I'd like—"

Charles waved further words aside. "Yes. Yes,
I know what you said," he said impatiently.
Then, rubbing his hand across his forehead, he
apologized for his tone. "Sorry, Inspector, I don't
know what came over me. I was fine until I sat
down."

"Delayed shock, I expect, sir."

"No, nothing like that," said Charles, shaking
his head. "The trouble was, I started thinking. It
was the scent, you see."

"The scent, sir?"

"Yes. That Marion, or, Mrs. Bundy, wore tonight. Ashes of Roses. It brought back so many memories.''

Before the inspector could comment, Margaret bustled up to them. ''I've told Miss Hawsberry to set up a cold buffet in the dining room. I don't know if anyone really feels like eating, but we should still offer something.''

Her cousin looked up. ''Thank you, Margaret. You always were the practical thinker. Oh, and be sure to tell the others not to leave afterward. The inspector wants to ask some questions.''

''Yes, of course,'' said Margaret. ''Oh, and Charles, I do think it would be a good idea to put out something stronger than sherry . . . but new bottles, please, and I'll keep an eye on them.'' She looked at the inspector. ''I'll feel much safer that way!''

MARION BUNDY DIED two hours later, without regaining consciousness, and an immediate autopsy was ordered. It had taken the inspector and Sergeant Buckingham less than two hours to ask the routine questions.

''How long do you know . . . ?''
''What did you see . . . ?''
''When was the last . . . ?''
''Where did she . . . ?''

And again, it was a matter of routine that after the questioning came the real work of comparing statements and trying to sort out any innocent remark that might give them a lead. Finally Sergeant Buckingham stole a look at his watch. Twelve-twenty. He made no attempt to stifle a noisy yawn. All the guests had left quite a while ago. Miss Twickham first, having been driven by Franks to the train station, would now be well on her way to the wedding in her home town, while the others would be snug in their beds. The sergeant heaved a sigh of self-pity.

The inspector looked up over his reading glasses. "Feeling a bit fagged, are you, Bucks? Don't worry, it shouldn't take much longer. Let's go over the statements once more, then take time off for a little well-deserved sleep. . .and I'd like to know what's holding up that lab report on Alicia Rochmere and the figurine," he added.

"Dr. Striker left word not to be disturbed, sir," said the sergeant, referring to a reply he'd got on his third attempt to reach the forensic laboratory.

Now it was the inspector's turn to sigh. "Ah, well, all in good time," he said resignedly. "He'll telephone as soon as he knows, but I've a feeling a lot is going to hinge on his findings. It's taking him a surprisingly long time to come up with a report." He leaned back in the chair. "Since there's nothing we can do about it, we might as well carry on as best we can, so let's hear what we have so far."

The inspector folded his hands across his stomach and closed his eyes as Sergeant Buckingham dutifully began reading from his notes.

"Mr. Trask certainly wasn't much help, sir. He'd never met Miss Rochmere and was only introduced to Mrs. Bundy tonight. The only comment he had was that he thought Mrs. Bundy was a striking-looking woman, and he, like everyone else, said she appeared slightly intoxicated. Mrs. Loft, on the other hand, was never even introduced to Mrs. Bundy. She was in the library when the victim arrived, and when she and Miss Cathcart went back into the drawing room, no one thought to correct this oversight—'' the sergeant cleared his throat ''—or there wasn't time. Mrs. Loft also stated that she did not know Miss Rochmere. Now Miss Emily King knew both ladies, but only slightly, from contact in the shop. Mr. Knight introduced them both to her at one time or another. However, all three—Mr. Trask, Mrs. Loft and Miss King—emphatically state that they had never had any social contact with either of the victims before tonight.'' The sergeant paused, waiting for comment, but since there was none forthcoming from the chair, he continued, ''Miss Twickham, although she's been here for twelve years, knew Mrs. Bundy only as a customer—they didn't move in the same social circle. Miss Rochmere, however, she knew a little better. They saw and spoke to each other at church every Sunday and often walked back to the High Street together. She says, however, that they never discussed anything personal, only generalities.''

''A genuine person, that Miss Twickham,'' said the inspector. ''Even though she didn't know the victims too well, she was truly upset by their demise. Quite the opposite of that other woman.''

''Uh, you mean Miss Purdy, sir?''

''I do. Odd, isn't it, that she, knowing both victims, didn't have more sympathy. In fact, as I recall, she was rather emphatic over her dislike of Mrs. Bundy.''

The sergeant consulted his notes. ''She expressed sorrow over Miss Rochmere's death, sir. Said they worked together at the church and missionary society; but it's true, she certainly wasn't sorry about Mrs. Bundy. Her exact words, in fact were, 'I did not like her in the least. I will not be a hypocrite and say I'm sorry she is dead. Quite the contrary. I'm very happy to be rid of her.' ''

"Quite a coldhearted statement, eh, Bucks?"

"Then, of course, there's her brother. . . ."

"My God, yes. But he's so far from reality, he wouldn't know how to deal with it if it were put on his doorstep!"

Sergeant Buckingham sighed. "And he was certainly in fine form tonight, sir. We couldn't even get a direct answer from him. All he kept ranting about was evil at work, sins of the fathers, possession by the Devil. . . . I think he's truly sick."

"Sick enough to be our murderer?" queried his superior.

Sergeant Buckingham considered the question carefully. "Perhaps. But I'm not going to commit myself as yet, sir."

The inspector nodded approvingly. "A wise man. But we're getting off the track." He massaged the back of his neck. "What else do we have?"

Sergeant Buckingham once again looked at his notes. "Miss Elizabeth Cathcart and Colonel Hawkins gave much the same story. They said that the Purdys moved away from Kingscombe when they were in their teens and no one thought much about them until Richard Purdy was transferred here by the church. His sister came with him to keep house. That was six years ago. Miss Rochmere was the daughter of the local vicar and led a rather secluded life—devoted it to looking after her father when he retired and moved to Ledbury Lane. After the death of her father, she spent her time growing prize roses in that walled garden of hers and doing church work. She wasn't too sociable outside the

church, so the others didn't see her very often.
Now Mrs. Bundy, on the other hand, remained a
very good friend, often coming to dinner and
meeting in the same social circles. Both the colonel and Miss Elizabeth Cathcart said she was
charming, witty and beautiful, but that she was
very hardheaded when it came to business. However, they couldn't imagine anyone hating her to
the point of murder.''

"And what did the other Miss Cathcart have to
say?'' asked the inspector.

"Miss Margaret Cathcart didn't agree at all, sir,
especially with the part about Mrs. Bundy having
no enemies. In her words, 'Marion had a very
strong personality. . . at times she could be quite
ruthless and not only in business matters. One
either had to accept her at face value or forever
be at loggerheads. I can't truthfully say, Sergeant, that I really liked her.' '' The sergeant
looked up from his notes.

"I can see why she didn't like her, Bucks,'' said
the inspector dryly. "When you think about it,
Miss Margaret Cathcart has a very similar personality to the one she just described.''

"You could be right,'' agreed Sergeant Buckingham. "She said another very interesting
thing, too. Apparently the plants in Marion Bundy's greenhouse were destroyed by vandals a
few nights ago—''

"Oh, yes.'' The inspector's brows drew together
in a puzzled frown. "Hmm. . . and Alicia Rochmere's flower garden was destroyed, as well.
Surely to heaven we don't have some nut running
about destroying his potential victims' gardens
before he strikes. We'd better check out that
story, Bucks. Anything else?''

Sergeant Buckingham tugged at his lower lip

and glanced at his notes again. "One thing they all agreed on was that Mrs. Bundy used to have one of the happiest marriages around here and no one seems to know exactly why her husband left."

"Ah, yes," said the inspector. "The elusive Mr. Bundy."

"I've contacted Central for a trace to be put on him, sir, and I also requested a rundown on all those present this afternoon and evening."

"Good. And we mustn't forget Miss Margaret Cathcart's revealing statement that Mrs. Bundy said she was to meet someone tonight."

Once more, the sergeant consulted his notes. "'An old love, a very dear and old love,' were Mrs. Bundy's words, sir, according to Miss Cathcart."

"I know," said the inspector, "and who could that old love be? At any rate, I've told Margaret Cathcart to keep it quiet for the present."

"I'm sure she will, sir," said Buckingham.

The inspector made no comment but simply looked critically at the circles and linking lines he'd been doodling on a pad of ruled paper. "Eenie Meenie Miney, Mo...."

"I beg pardon, sir?"

"I said, Eenie, Meenie, Miney, Mo. You know, the game children play? Who's going to be 'it'?" He tossed the pad across to the other side of the desk. "Take your pick, Bucks. Which one did them in?"

The sergeant looked at the interlinking circles. "Oh, oh yes, I see what you mean, sir—" The jangling of the telephone cut him short.

"Chief Inspector Dobbs."

"Bob Striker, here, Ronald," an excited voice

said. "I've completed the report on Alicia Roch-mere."

"And about time, too!" boomed the inspector.

"Sorry, Ronald, but it took us a while to track down the poison."

The inspector groaned. "I've a feeling I'm not going to like it."

"And I've a feeling you're right," said Dr. Striker. "It's something we've never come across—not in murder, anyway. It's a chemical used in insecticides. Parathion."

The inspector grunted noncommittally. "I've heard of it. Should take all the damn insecticides off the market."

"I agree wholeheartedly, Ronald, but that wasn't what was used."

"What do you mean, man? You just said it was parathion!"

"That's right. But not an insecticide. An insec-ticide contains less than 2% parathion, which can be lethal enough, but it looks like your murderer, Ronald, used it in its pure undiluted state."

The inspector's chair shot into an upright posi-tion. "Do you mean to say we have someone going around with pure parathion in their possession?"

"I'm afraid that's exactly what I mean."

"But where could they get it?"

"I've already done your homework for you, Ronald. About eight months ago, a shipment of this stuff was on its way to Scotland. When it ar-rived, a five-gallon drum was missing. The route was immediately retraced and scoured, of course, but to no avail. Questions were asked, discreetly, and no one knew anything. Finally it was officially decided that perhaps a mistake had been made and the invoice showed one drum too many. It was one of those sticky situations where you aren't sure whether to inform the public or not—you remember that hue and cry about nerve gases being shipped last year—so it was decided to keep this incident under wraps.''

"I recall it now," said the inspector.

"Yes. Well, I wanted to make absolutely sure, so I called Central, and I was right. The missing drum contained pure parathion.''

"Good God!''

"And I'm afraid nothing else of any importance has shown up that can be of help. No prints on the figurine other than those that we've matched up with the victim's. The letters pasted on the outside of the box were neatly cut from a woman's weekly that can be purchased at any news agency. The box, paper and string can be bought at any variety store, and as far as the card is concerned, it's an ordinary file card. The type on the card is from a Royal typewriter with the lower case 'e' slightly out of line. That's our best clue, so far, but I've a feeling that our murderer is not so stupid as to use a typewriter that's within a fifty-mile radius. At this moment, the only thing I *can* say about your man—or woman—is that he's neat. Those letters clipped from the magazine were meticulously trimmed and the typing on the card was centered exactly." He paused. "You better catch this murderer, soon, Ronald, otherwise. . . .''

The inspector sighed. "Bob," he said tiredly, "we already have a second murder. You'll have the body at your lab any time now. I sent over a glass and some bottles, as well.''

"Haven't seen them yet," he said. "Been too busy. I'll get at it immediately. I'll be in touch.

Shouldn't take long, now that we know what to look for.'' The phone went dead.

By the time the inspector related the lab findings, Sergeant Buckingham was no longer feeling drowsy.

"Now, where would you hide a five-gallon drum of parathion, Bucks? It has to be easily accessible and yet in a place where no one might stumble across it.''

"Sir, I wouldn't hazard a guess. . . and yet I can think of hundreds of places where it might be.''

"Exactly. So let's get some men working on it,'' said the inspector determinedly. He reached for the telephone and began making arrangements.

Listening to his superior's ever-so-explicit instructions that the searchers exercise discretion—they didn't want their murderer to push the panic button—Sergeant Buckingham felt a chill run through him. When the inspector put down the phone, the sergeant couldn't help but comment, "He must be a raving maniac.''

"Maniacal, yes, but far from raving. Cunning would be more the right word. That's why I find it hard to believe he'd bother destroying gardens,'' said the inspector. He leaned back in the chair and once again closed his eyes in thought. "My God, Bucks. What a dirty business we're in. All we look for is the putridity in people—some rotten thing they did to make some rotten person want to kill. And of all the ways to kill, I hate a poisoning the most because it's obviously the tool of a premeditated murder and we have to dig.'' He ran his hand through his hair, contemplating the task ahead. "God, how we have to dig. It's not like a shooting or a knifing. I mean, a gun or

knife very often means the killing was done in
the rage of the moment, not that it makes any
difference to the poor bloody victim but more
often than not we have to retrace only a short
distance. But poison...that, Bucks, is used by a
cold, calculating, gutless individual who won't
even face his—"

He stopped in midsentence, as a thought suddenly struck. He shook his head. "You know,
Bucks, somehow this just doesn't connect. Both
victims were poisoned. Alicia Rochmere was definitely the intended victim—the package containing the poison was delivered directly to her.
But what about Marion Bundy? Was she the right
victim? How could the murderer be sure she'd
choose that particular glass of sherry? How could
it have been poisoned when she had it in her
hand for only a few minutes?" He shook his head
again, frowning. "No, Bucks, somewhere our
thinking is definitely off."

About an hour passed before Inspector Dobbs
and Sergeant Buckingham were again interrupted by the ringing of the telephone.

It was the pathologist again, with the autopsy
report on Marion Bundy, and for a full three minutes the inspector listened. Finally, with a
"Thank you, Bob," he slammed down the receiver while at the same time getting to his feet. "Get
your coat on, Bucks," he said, throwing the sergeant his mac from the coatrack. "We're going to
Redwing. I've just learned that Marion Bundy
didn't *drink* the poison; she *absorbed* it through
the skin!"

"But I don't understand....."

By now the sergeant was hastening to keep up
with his superior in the hall.

"Neither do I, and that's not all I don't understand. For some reason she and her disappearing husband hoodwinked everyone in the village about their idyllic marriage."

"How's that, sir?"

"Mrs. Bundy died a virgin, Bucks," said the inspector, jamming his hat on his head as he bent his tall frame into the police car.

THIS TIME it was Sergeant Rawlins who met them at the door. He and Constable Reed had been sent to the Bundy house to question the servants and conduct a search through desks and drawers in hopes of finding a reason for Mrs. Bundy's poisoning. They were about to call it a night, when the inspector's car pulled up. Earlier, the sergeant had phoned the Hall to say that the stable lads had readily cooperated, although as far as he could see, their answers shed no light. Mrs. Bundy was not one to befriend her employees. Ben Dawson directed all the outside work, and so long as the jobs were done, Marion Bundy took no interest in the people who did them. The cook, a taciturn sort of woman, had grudgingly answered their questions, but she, too, was of little help, telling them she took no notice of anything outside the kitchen. It was Grace Dawson, the young maid, however, who was giving them troubles. On hearing of her mistress's death, she'd promptly gone into hysterics and they couldn't get any sense out of her. The inspector had told Sergeant Rawlins to let her be—he'd see her in the morning—and to get on with their searching. That, of course, was before he'd received Dr. Striker's report.

Any leniency he'd extended was forgotten, as

he burst into the kitchen to find a now pampered
Grace thoroughly enjoying the mollycoddling
lavished upon her by her family, rallied around
their poor chick in her time of need. On second
glance, not only family, but Colonel Hawkins's
chauffeur, Frank Franks was there—silly sort of
tag, thought the inspector; what the devil was he
doing there, anyway? It didn't take him long to
sort out the fact that, like the family, the boy-
friend had answered the call of a female in distress. The time to cater to hysterics was past,
however. And with a glower, the inspector sent
them packing—all except Grace, who instinctively knew better than to try for any more sympathy.
Ten minutes later, the mysterious bottle Grace
had found in a package at the door and had subsequently put on the shelf in the bathroom was
being rushed to the laboratory, carefully sealed in
a plastic bag as little Angelique had been.

Questioned at length, the maid was no help.
No, she hadn't seen who'd left the package. She
found it when she swept the front steps, a task
she performed every morning. Was it sealed?
Mailed? No, to both accounts. Loosely wrapped
in brown paper, the package had no name or address; that's why she'd opened it. Only the card
inside had Mrs. Bundy's name on it. The bottle
was tied wtih a pretty bow—as if from a friend,
thought Grace. She'd put it on the shelf and forgotten all about it, what with Miss Rochmere's
death and all. . . . The paper wrapping? Taken
out with the trash that morning.

"Are these *all* the fruits of your search, Sergeant Rawlins?" asked the inspector, indicating
several cardboard accordion files sitting on the
table.

"Yes, sir. Unlike Miss Rochmere, Mrs. Bundy kept everything neat and orderly—checks, receipts, all nicely filed."

"Hmm," said the inspector, sipping the coffee that the cook had ungraciously condescended to make. "And where did you find *this*?"

He indicated a metal box that sat conspicuously in the center of the table.

"In the bottom of the large wardrobe in Mrs. Bundy's room. The key was hanging on a hook on the inside of the wardrobe door. I was on my way to the Hall with it when you arrived."

"Well, let's open it. However, I don't expect the murderer's name to leap out at me. I've had my quota of surprises for the day," said the inspector sardonically.

The inspector was right. The box contained no picture or name of a possible murderer. Only old bankbooks. But he had been wrong about his quota of surprises. It didn't take him long to determine that it was Marion Bundy whom Alicia Rochmere had blackmailed for nineteen years!

7

EMILY DIDN'T KNOW what woke her. It was pitch-black and a few seconds passed before her mind oriented itself and she realized she was in her own bed at Rose Hill. Then she heard the voices of a man and a woman. The tones were angry, but so low, she could discern only a phrase here and there.

"...I didn't know...be all right...."

"...shouldn't have done it...."

"...there's no harm...."

"...warning you...have no idea...."

"...know what I'm doing...."

Then in a fit of temper, the man's voice shouted, "Don't try it again!"

With a start, she realized it was John's voice. She looked at the bedside clock. Two o'clock. He'd left her at the front door more than an hour ago! She'd stood and waved goodbye as he'd set off for his room at the Fox and Hound, with a promise to see her at breakfast in the morning. Now here he was back again, and obviously he and Sarah were having an argument. Over what?

She suddenly recalled Sarah's odd remark as they'd stood by the stricken Marion in the colonel's drawing room. Had that something to do with the quarrel? She shook her head. No, that was silly. She hadn't even mentioned the comment to John. In fact, with all the goings-on, she'd quite forgotten about it until this moment. There probably was a simple explanation. She listened intently, straining to hear the conversation. But after that one outburst, the voices were even lower than before and now she could not detect even simple phrases.

Fifteen minutes later, the front door slammed and she heard the roar of a car's engine. For a long while she lay there, thoughts flashing through her mind, none of them making any sense. When finally she did drift off to sleep, the sky was beginning to lighten.

The wind had died during the night and the day held promise of being warm and sunny. Looking into the mirror, Emily saw dark circles under her eyes, but with expert makeup application, they soon disappeared. She was still in a quandary about the night before when she came downstairs and found Sarah and John having breakfast on the terrace.

"Good morning, my dear. Did you sleep well?" John asked, bussing the top of her head as he pushed the chair in for her.

Emily looked up at him and then across at Sarah. Both were smiling, poised expectantly for her answer. What should she say? What would they say if they knew she'd heard the argument? Instead of a direct reply, Emily countered with a question. "Did *you* sleep well, Sarah? After all the excitement?" She saw a look, brief though it was, pass between aunt and nephew.

Sarah laughed shortly. "Like a baby. Best sleep I've had in months!" she said brightly. Well, that certainly told Emily what track to take.

"Me, too," she lied. "It must have been all that

fresh air from our drive last night. I was asleep as soon as I hit the pillow. Didn't hear a thing till my alarm this morning.''

Their relief was almost tangible.

"I'm glad you had a good sleep. After the other night, you needed one," said Sarah. She looked at her nephew. "Did Emily tell you about the nightmare she had Friday night, John?"

John sat down to Emily's left. "Yes, she did, before we went to the Hall last evening. It gave her a bad scare. She can't imagine what caused it."

Watching the two of them, Emily was sure that a silent message once more flashed between John and his aunt.

"You two must have gone for a long drive," said Sarah. "I know I didn't hear you come in, Emily, and I turned off my light at midnight."

"We drove into Torbay and stopped for a night-cap at a club," said John, helping himself to the toast.

Emily took her cue. If this was the way they wanted it so be it; three could play the game as well as two. "Then I asked John to stop at the Bell on the way home," said Emily. "I wanted to pick up the doll I'd promised to deliver to Colonel Hawkins last night, but with all the commotion yesterday, I forgot all about it. He was very disappointed, so I promised to drop it off first thing today."

"I asked her to wait until this morning to pick it up," said John, "but she insisted she'd sleep better having known she'd done her duty."

"I can well understand that," said Sarah, "and from the way she looks this morning, her idea worked."

Emily shivered. What was she doing in this charade? She was being swept along against her will. "After we'd gone in, I wished I'd taken John's advice. Even with him there, it was creepy! I didn't spend any more time than I had to...simply picked up the doll and grabbed a piece of paper to wrap it in. All I could think of was poor Miss Rochmere lying there on the floor."

"Umm," mumbled John, munching toast. "Pass the marmalade, will you please, Sarah?"

"What are you planning for the day?" asked his aunt, handing him the quince conserve.

"After Emily performs her task, I thought we might drive along the sea road and stop for a swim somewhere. How's that sound to you?" he asked, turning toward Emily.

"Lovely," she said weakly. Yesterday, the idea of being afraid of John would never have entered her head, but now...

"Well, for goodness' sake, be careful. There's a murderer about, you know."

"No need to be reminded," said John grimly.

"You'll be back for tea?" asked Sarah.

John smiled at his aunt. "Of course. On the dot of six. Simply because I have a lovely lady to squire around, it doesn't mean I'll neglect my favorite aunt."

"Flatterer!" snorted Sarah, rising from her chair. "Now if you both will excuse me, I think I'll go to my room and get my thoughts in order. Have a nice day...and be careful." This last was directed solely at her nephew. Concern, thought Emily, or could it be a warning? Whichever, John chose to take it lightheartedly.

"I always am, aunt," he said, taking her elbow

and helping her toward her room. "The trouble with you is that you consider driving over twenty miles an hour guilty of speeding."

"You know that's not true." She looked over her shoulder. "Emily, don't listen to him. He makes me sound feeble-minded. And I can fend for myself, thank you," Sarah said, shaking off her nephew's helping hand. "I'll see you both at six."

"Your wish is my command," said John with a mock bow. He came over and leaning both hands on the table, looked directly into Emily's green eyes. "And now, Emily, dear, if you'll hurry up and finish your breakfast, we'll drive to the Hall and then have a lovely day by the sea."

THE CATHCART SISTERS had been in Elizabeth's room for the past half hour, discussing the possible whys and wherefores of the two murders and getting exactly nowhere. Elizabeth, sitting by the window, watched her sister wear a path between the bed and the fireplace.

"Will you sit down!"

"What do you think of her?" asked Margaret, not breaking her stride.

Elizabeth looked blank. This was another of Margaret's most annoying habits—expecting one to know exactly whom or what she was talking about, when she threw out a query entirely out of context.

"Who?" she demanded.

"Sarah Loft, of course!" cried Margaret in exasperation.

"Don't get so excited, dear. The world hasn't come to an end," said Elizabeth placidly. "I can't say I formed any real opinion of her, other than that she's grossly overweight. We only exchanged a few words. Charles introduced us when they came in. I met her nephew and secretary, too, and I thought they made a lovely couple. Didn't you?''

"Yes, yes," said Margaret, treading back and forth, "but I'm not interested in them. *She's* the one who intrigues me. As I told Charles, a writer who won't talk about her work is not to be believed."

"Well," said her sister dubiously, "I suppose there are a few, er, oddballs?''

"Oh, no doubt," agreed Margaret. "But that's not all that bothers me. There's something else.... I don't know precisely what it is that keeps nagging at the back of my mind ever since I saw her last night. I just can't put my finger on it."

"I don't see how you ever will, dear, pacing the floor like a caged animal. Sometimes if you think too hard for an answer, you never get it. Why don't you put it out of your mind and go for a leisurely stroll? I can assure you that the answer will come all the sooner."

Margaret changed her course and headed toward the door. "You're probably right, Elizabeth. I woke up at five this morning with the problem on my mind and I haven't let go. Now I'll forget about it entirely," she said with resolution.

THE ROAR OF A CAR ENGINE caused Margaret to quickly step off the gravel onto the grassy verge. A blue Ford rounded the bend in the driveway and squealed to a stop, and two smiling faces looked up at her... well, one smiling face. Margaret noticed that Emily's smile did not reach her eyes.

"Good morning, Miss Cathcart," said John.

Ignoring the civilities, Margaret accosted the driver. "John Trask! You frightened me out of ten years' growth."

The young man behind the wheel laughed. "Sorry. I admit I do get carried away at times."

"Well do try to remember this isn't the Grand Prix, please. We've been shaken out of our tranquillity quite enough during the past twenty-four hours."

"Couldn't agree with you more," said John, "and I apologize. Now, can we give you a lift?"

"No, thanks. You're heading in the opposite direction. I'm going down to the museum. By the way, if you wanted to see my cousin, you're out of luck. He went into Exeter today. He should be back soon, however."

"Oh, dear," said Emily, picking up her parcel. "I had this doll to give him."

"Is that the one you mended?" asked Margaret. "Give it to me, and I'll take it down to the coach house."

"Would you? I'd appreciate it," said Emily, handing over the package.

"Then we *are* going in the same direction," said John, reaching for the door.

"No, we aren't. It's a lovely day for walking and I'm going to cut through the woods. It takes longer, but it's more pleasant. Thanks, anyway."

"I know when I'm defeated," said the young man.

"Miss Cathcart—" began Emily.

"We're taking a drive along the coast and perhaps we'll stop for a swim," interjected John.

"Beautiful day for it, don't you think?" He put the car into gear and it began to move.

Left with nothing else to say, Margaret called, "Have a nice day."

As the machine was expertly maneuvered around, Emily halfheartedly waved goodbye.

Thoughtfully, Margaret listened to the receding engine. What had Emily wanted to say? And why had John cut her off? She liked these two people and it disturbed her to see them obviously at odds with each other. The sudden shriek of a bird cutting through the stillness brought her out of her thoughts with a start, and unselfconsciously she laughed aloud. What earthly concern was it of hers anyway? Lovers' tiffs were nothing unusual, and from all reports she'd heard, were often rather satisfyingly patched up. Purposefully, she set off on her mission to the coach house.

When she reached it, the door was wide open to the spring air, and an off-key voice was attempting to sing a current pop tune. Stepping inside and putting her package on a nearby table, Margaret waited until her eyes became adjusted to the light. Still she could see no one. Following the course set by her ear, ahead and to the right, she came upon a woman in a flowered coverall kneeling by a mock battlefield, engrossed in polishing the tiny figures of toy soldiers. "Good morning," she said.

Startled, the woman gasped and scurried to her feet. "My, you startled me. I didn't hear anyone come in."

Margaret smiled and propped herself on the edge of a low table. "I'm sorry," she said and, recalling her encounter in the library the previous night, added, "I seem to have a knack lately of coming upon people unexpectedly. I didn't know anyone would be here. My sister and I arrived from London yesterday. I'm Margaret Cathcart."

The other woman nodded in acknowledgment. "I'm Ruth Dawson."

It was Margaret's turn to be surprised. "Mrs. Dawson! I didn't know you were employed by my cousin!"

"Just since the colonel turned this into a museum. When it's open, I'll come in once a week to see to the polishing but right now I try to spend an hour or so a day here, getting things in shape for the grand opening."

"You have a niece and nephew who work at Redwing, don't you?"

Mrs. Dawson beamed, pleased that Margaret should take an interest in her family. "That's right, although I don't know what's going to happen now that Mrs. Bundy's gone."

Margaret dropped her smile. "Tragic, wasn't it? And Miss Rochmere the same day."

"That it was," agreed the loquacious Mrs. Dawson. "My brother sent his boy over to get us—Grace had hysterics, and she doesn't have a mother. I'll tell you, Miss Cathcart, it took us a good while to get her calmed down. In truth, if it hadn't been for that young man, Franks, who works for Colonel Hawkins, I don't think we could ever have stopped her crying and carrying on. He was a mountain of strength, and that's a fact. But we just got her calmed down when that inspector came barging in and started asking more questions. That's why I'm keeping busy here on a Sunday. I'm a nervous wreck, what with police in and out of the house all night."

"They were there all night?"

"Until dawn. And when they found that bottle...."

"What bottle?" asked Margaret, trying to suppress her excitement. "I haven't heard anything about a bottle."

Margaret's implication that she'd like to hear more was fuel for Mrs. Dawson's fire. She was only too happy to relate the previous night's events, enlarging pleasurably on the details as Margaret gave appreciative ohs and ahs. Mrs. Dawson just "happened" to be near the door when the inspector questioned Grace. She just "happened" to walk into the kitchen (Grace needed a cup of coffee) when the police were going through a metal box found in Mrs. Bundy's room—of course, they'd stopped talking when she came in, but there were several bankbooks laid out on the table, and there was no denying the police were excited. As for the bottle they found in Mrs. Bundy's bathroom...well, she definitely did hear them say there was no doubt it contained the poison. Mrs. Dawson "happened" to be standing on the landing as they came down the stairs.

Fifteen minutes later, Margaret felt that Ruth Dawson was indeed a powerful ally, but she didn't feel she could push her any further and ask questions about Sarah Loft. She'd save that for later. "It's appalling that these things have to happen," said Margaret.

"What makes it even worse is that it's so out of place in a village like Kingscombe. Who'd ever suspect so much hate was here? We're quiet and peacefullike," said Mrs. Dawson. "We mind our own business." (Margaret had doubts about that.) Mrs. Dawson furrowed her brow in reflection. "Of course, there was Mr. Bundy who ran off; that stirred up some fur, I can tell you. But aside from that, we've always been a decent lot...except for Eunice Freeman, who had to leave because she was in the family way; as my dear old Mum used to say, 'good riddance to bad rubbish.' Hoity-toity lot if ever there was one," said Mrs. Dawson, kneeling down again on the floor.

"I'm sure every village has such incidents," remarked Margaret.

"Oh, I'm sure they do, Miss Cathcart." Ruth Dawson dipped her cloth into the polish. "I'm sorry, but you don't mind if I get on with this, do you? I don't mean to be rude, but I'd like to get it finished."

"No, no, it's quite all right," said Margaret, walking toward the door. "I've disrupted your work quite enough. Thanks again for your time," she called from the doorway. There was no response. Mrs. Dawson was deeply engrossed in her polishing task.

The day had turned very warm, and as Margaret made her way to the harbor, she shed her coat and carried it over her arm. Lost in thought, as she hashed over Mrs. Dawson's story of the previous night, she was surprised to hear her name called. Looking up, she found herself standing by the gate of Rose Hill. Sarah Loft was beckoning to her from the garden seat. One of the last people Margaret expected to find there was George Knight, seated next to her, looking very ill at ease.

"Do come and join us, won't you?" called Sarah. "We're just sitting here enjoying the warmth of the sun."

Margaret pushed open the gate. "I didn't expect to find you out here! I thought you always wrote in the afternoon? At least, that's what Emily told me."

Sarah laughed. "So I do, and was, until George came banging at my door and wouldn't cease until it was opened." Under the scrutiny of her brown eyes, the little man squirmed uncomfortably. "As it turns out he wanted Emily, but of course, she isn't here, and since he disturbed my train of thought, I decided to punish him by making him stay and join me in a chat. Speaking of trains of thought, by the way, you were most engrossed in yours, Margaret. I had to call your name twice before you heard me."

"I'm sorry. I was thinking about a conversation I just had with your housekeeper, Mrs. Dawson."

"Goodness!" exclaimed Sarah. "Not about me, I hope. At least, I'd hate to think anything said about me would cause such retrospect."

Margaret laughed. "No. Your name wasn't even mentioned. As a matter of fact, we were mostly discussing the police work." She looked at the antique dealer. "I'm sure you've heard about Marion's death, George?"

The little man nodded. "Terrible! Amy Purdy told me this morning," he said, producing a white handkerchief from his breast pocket and daintily patting his brow. "What a dreadful thing to have happened! Poison in her drink!"

Margaret didn't feel there was any reason to enlighten them about the mysterious bottle.

"Have the police made any progress, do you know?" asked Sarah.

"I couldn't say, and the inspector doesn't appear to me to be the type to confide in women.

Personally, I think he's rather a grouch. Anyway, I haven't seen him nor his sergeant this morning. Aside from Mrs. Dawson, the only other two people I've met are John and Emily."

"That's right," said Sarah. "Emily was taking a doll to Colonel Hawkins."

"Well, I met them on the driveway to the house, and since Charles wasn't home and I was on my way to the museum, I delivered her package for her."

Both Sarah and Margaret turned toward Mr. Knight as the little man noisily caught his breath. "You took it to the museum for her?" he yelped.

"Yes. Why? Wasn't it supposed to go there?" asked Margaret, concerned that she may have done the wrong thing.

"No! Er...yes!" stammered the little man, taking off his pince-nez and rubbing the lenses vigorously with his handkerchief. "It's just... I...I hope she had it well wrapped," he said, adjusting the glasses on his nose.

"Of course, it was in paper," said Margaret. "I'm surprised at you, George," she admonished, "thinking Emily wouldn't know enough to protect a fragile antique. You should be ashamed of yourself!"

"I know, I know," he said, holding up his hand to ward off any further admonitions, "and I'm sorry. But as you pointed out, it *is* fragile! Uh... where did you put it, by the way? Some place safe, I hope? I'm going over later to set up a few more exhibits and I'll put it in the case."

"Right on the table to the left of the door as you come in. You can't miss it," said Margaret, "and there's no one there to disturb it except Mrs. Dawson...who just might take a notion to open it, considering her curiosity," she added teasingly. She was immediately sorry she'd been so guileless. The antique dealer was now perspiring freely and his skin had taken on a waxen sheen. "Are you all right, George?"

The little man jumped up, mopping his face. "I...I'm fine, thank you, Margaret. Sorry I'm so jittery. Must be delayed shock from yesterday... or perhaps something I ate.... I really don't feel very well."

"How terrible!" exclaimed Sarah, "and I don't have a car."

Margaret looked at her watch. "I could see if Charles is home—"

"No! No, that won't be necessary," said the rotund little man nervously. "I can make it home. It isn't far."

"I'll walk with you," said Margaret.

"It's simply nerves, I tell you," squeaked the little man, loosening his tie. "Please stop making a fuss! I'll be fine when I get home!"

"Well, I'm seeing that you do get home," said Margaret. "What's more, I'm going to make you a good strong cup of tea and pour some of that brandy into it."

Confronted by two determined women, George Knight had no choice but to succumb to their demands. Obediently he leaned on Margaret's sturdy arm.

"I've rung Fred Cotes, but he's at the hospital," said Margaret, tucking a blanket around her charge. "Thank heavens Charles is back now and is sending Franks 'round with the car."

"This is nonsense, you know," protested the sick man. "It's simply a case of nerves. I've had bouts of this before . . . and I don't need a doctor. When you leave, I'll go to bed and rest for an hour or so.''

Margaret shook her head. "It's more than nerves, George. You're positively green around the gills and I'm not leaving you until you see the doctor. Now drink this tea. I didn't put brandy in it in case he prescribes drugs. Heaven knows you look as if you need medicine.''

The man propped up in the armchair was in no condition to argue. He simply waved the tea away and leaned back with his eyes closed. ''Perhaps you're right,'' he murmured.

Several minutes later the ringing of the doorbell announced Franks's arrival. He and Margaret helped George Knight into the car.

Dr. Cotes's diagnosis took only a short time. Leaving the patient in the capable hands of a nurse, he stepped out into the hall and beckoned to Margaret. "An acute case of the flu on top of poor physical condition. I'm going to keep him here a few days.''

''You're sure it's not . . . ?''

''Poison?'' finished the doctor. ''No. I'm quite sure.''

''Thank heavens,'' breathed Margaret. ''Oh, I must phone Sarah Loft and tell her about George. I'm sure the same thought crossed her mind.''

''Fine. I'll take care of the admitting.''

Sarah's voice revealed first anxiety and then relief at Margaret's news. Her reaction to George Knight's being admitted to the hospital, however, took Margaret unaware. Thoughtfully replacing the receiver, she retracked the conversation. Was it her imagination, or had Sarah actually sounded pleased when told that George would be in hospital for at least several days?

She walked over to the desk where the doctor was filling out forms. "Fred, what do you think of Sarah Loft?"

Dr. Cotes shrugged. "I never gave her much thought. Speaking strictly as a physician, though, I can tell you she'd better watch her blood pressure and take off some of that weight, or she'll end up as a patient." The doctor frowned. "As a matter of fact, I'm surprised she isn't already my patient. She came to Kingscombe primarily for her health and I should think her own doctor in London would have told her at least to have monthly checkups. Obesity, at her age, is something you don't fool around with."

"Perhaps she goes back to London for these checkups."

"You're probably right," agreed the doctor. "Anyway, it really doesn't become my problem until I'm invited."

They began walking down the hall. "What particularly interests me," said Margaret, "are her clothes. She certainly doesn't try to minimize her size."

The doctor laughed. "You find that strange? Did you ever think it might be because she's embarrassed? Let me tell you something. From the little psychology I took in medical school, I did retain a few lessons, and one was that many people with inferiority complexes tend to flaunt their faults. They get more attention that way."

"And you think Sarah Loft has an inferiority complex?"

"No, I'm just saying it's a possibility."

"Well, I think you're wrong," said Margaret. "There's nothing inferior about that one."

They were now at the hospital exit and Fred Cotes hastily reached out to push open the door. As Margaret passed him, he tentatively touched her arm.

"Margaret," he said, "I know how determined you can be and I'll give you a bit of advice, something an old professor said to me when I was a cocky med student. I've always remembered it. 'What you see is not always what you *think* you see.' Keeping that thought in mind has more than once served its purpose since I hung out my shingle."

"I'll remember that," she said, "but I still don't think Sarah Loft's hiding an inferiority complex!" Franks had the rear door open, but Margaret chose to ignore it and climbed into the front passenger seat. "I'll sit up here with you, Franks."

"Very well, madam." Gently he closed the door and got in behind the wheel.

For a few minutes they drove in silence, then Margaret could contain herself no longer. "Mrs. Dawson told me you were over at Redwing last night . . . because Grace was so upset."

"Mrs. Dawson had her nephew fetch me, in hopes I could calm her down some."

"Mrs. Dawson also mentioned a bottle. . . ."

"A bottle?"

"Yes. One the police found. Grace didn't happen to mention one, did she?"

A frown creased his forehead. "She wasn't talking much last night. More babbling and crying. Then just when we thought she'd come 'round, the inspector came in and upset her all over again.''

"Yes, I heard about that," said Margaret. "Poor little thing. I imagine he can be quite harsh. But never mind, she'll soon bounce back and be good as new. I was thinking that perhaps Mrs. Loft might employ her, now that Mrs. Dawson is busy with the museum. Does Grace like Mrs. Loft, do you know?"

Deftly, Franks guided the car around a sharp curve, while he appeared to be thinking of an appropriate answer. When it came, it was not what Margaret had expected. "Perhaps you should ask Grace, Miss Cathcart."

Glancing at the chauffeur, Margaret suddenly felt uncomfortable. She'd been subtly put in her place. She'd been prying and the young man wasn't going to let her get away with it. They drove in silence, Franks concentrating on the road and Margaret looking resignedly at the passing scenery. "There certainly aren't many people about," she observed at last. "Can't say as I blame them, with a murderer running amok."

Franks made no comment and the silence was becoming oppressive. Thank heaven, thought Margaret, that neither Charles nor Elizabeth was in the back seat to witness her discomfort. Come to think of it, if they had been in the back seat, she probably wouldn't be in this predicament. She cudgeled her brain for something to say—something innocuous that would warrant a reply. A thought struck her. "Are you from these parts, Franks?"

The chauffeur smiled disarmingly. Why did she feel they were playing cat and mouse?

"From London, madam."

For some reason she felt as though she should explain her question. "You don't have a definitive accent, you know. In fact, if I were asked, I suppose I should place you somewhere from Scotland."

"I've moved about a good deal—particularly as a boy."

"Oh, did your father's employment entail traveling?" No sooner were the words out than she knew she'd once again overstepped her bounds. Franks's scowl confirmed it.

"My father left my mother shortly after I was born."

"Oh! I *am* sorry," said a flustered Margaret.

"It's quite all right, madam. It's ancient history."

As they approached the pillars marking the entrance to the driveway of the Hall, she reached for the door handle. "I think I'll get out here and walk the rest of the way, Franks."

The chauffeur brought the car to a smooth halt and she stepped out. With a simple thank-you she closed the door. Walking up the driveway, she was furious with herself. How could she be so blundering? Two men today had put her in her place, and she wasn't used to that. Dr. Cotes's parting remark had really rankled. "What you see is not always what you think you see." Well, fine and dandy. She'd go along with that, but not in regard to Sarah Loft. There was definitely something there that troubled her; if only she could remember what it was!

She stumbled on a stone. Oh, bother! She was out of sorts with everything today. It was so hot. She never should have worn a long-sleeved blouse and most certainly not a coat! An unfamiliar weariness washed over her. The events of the past two days had caught up. Suddenly, she didn't want to return to the house and be with people. All she wanted at the moment was to be enveloped in this quiet solitude of the woods. Wending her way through the brush and trees, Margaret came across a small clearing. She was on the perimeter of a copse near the edge of a green meadow. The only sign of civilization was the chimney of the coach house peeping above the trees. She needed to relax, do some thinking. She spread her coat on the ground and sank down on it. Small puffs of cloud drifted gently against a blue sky, and sunlight created leafy lace patterns as it played through the trees. The silence was complete, broken only now and then by the cheerful chirping of a bird and the scurrying of squirrels. Margaret closed her eyes in sheer contentment.

A twig snapped. Then another. . . and another! Margaret sat bolt upright. Someone was running through the woods.

Instinctively, she was tempted to cry out, to ask who was there, but common sense stopped her. With a murderer loose, one didn't take chances. Straining, she listened for more telltale noises. Again several twigs snapped. Whoever it was wasn't making any effort to be quiet. And, thought Margaret, relief flowing through her, whoever it was obviously didn't know she was there. The noises began to fade. Finally, after several moments of silence, she cautiously stood up and gazed around. It was when she looked toward the meadow that a loud, involuntary gasp escaped her lips. There in the distance, hurrying along the footpath, in unmistakable long strides, was the figure of Miss Twickham.

For a moment, Margaret stood still, her mouth gaping; then she sat back down with a thump. It couldn't possibly be. Miss Twickham was up north! She stood and looked again, but the person had disappeared. Margaret forced herself to think logically. The runner had been to her right and the only thing on that side, other than trees and road, was the museum. Grabbing her coat, she made her way to the coach house, uncaring about snags or rents to her clothing. When she got there, Mrs. Dawson was standing on the step, about to close the door.

"Mrs. Dawson!" The cleaning woman turned around, her wide-eyed look causing Margaret to take stock of her attire.

Unsuccessfully patting her hair into place, she explained, "I had a fight with a bramble bush."

"I see," said Mrs. Dawson doubtfully.

"But that's neither here nor there," said Margaret, rushing on. "What I wanted to ask you is, have you seen Miss Twickham?"

"When?"

"Today!" said Margaret, more sharply than she intended.

Offended by the other's tone, Mrs. Dawson clamped her lips together. "There's no need to get excited, Miss Cathcart," she said in an injured voice.

"I'm sorry, Mrs. Dawson," said Margaret contritely. "You see, I thought I saw her a few minutes ago, coming from the museum, and I wanted to be certain. Did you see her?"

Mrs. Dawson peered more closely. "Are you sure you're all right, Miss Cathcart?"

"Of course I am," said Margaret impatiently.

Mrs. Dawson nodded. "I see," she said, clearly implying that she did not. "No, Miss Cathcart, I did not see Miss Twickham. In fact, no one's been here today except yourself. Did you forget Miss Twickham left last night for a wedding? Her cousin's minding the shop for a few days.''

"No, I didn't forget that she was going to catch the train; I simply thought that perhaps she'd missed it.''

Mrs. Dawson brightened. "Oh, well that would explain things, wouldn't it then? I suggest you go and see if she's home.'' She inserted the key in the lock.

"Don't do that!'' said Margaret, seizing her hand. Startled at Margaret's vehemence, Mrs. Dawson yanked her hand away, shrinking from any further contact.

Seeing the fear in the other woman's eyes brought Margaret to her senses. "I'm sorry, Mrs. Dawson, I didn't mean to sound so intense. I don't know what came over me. But you see,'' she tried to explain, "I thought I'd just take a look at the exhibits.''

Mrs. Dawson was not to be taken in. "I thought you had your own key,'' she said suspiciously. "You must have, if you intended to get in this morning.''

"How silly of me! Of course, I have,'' said Margaret, fishing in her pocket. "I'd forgotten all about it.''

Mrs. Dawson's opinion of Colonel Hawkins's cousin was definitely on the decline. With an abrupt nod, she started down the path, only too glad to get away.

"Mrs. Dawson!'' called Margaret, turning toward the hastily departing figure, "I know you're in a hurry to leave, but would you answer just one more question, please?''

Reluctantly, Mrs. Dawson looked back.

"I left a package on the little table by the door
this morning. It's a doll Miss King repaired. You
didn't move it by any chance, did you?" The in-
dignant look on Mrs. Dawson's face caused her to
rush on. "I mean, not that you shouldn't have,
but Mr. Knight hasn't cataloged it yet and he
asked me specifically where he'd find it."

"I don't know anything about a package. All I
attended to was my own work." Hurt by Margaret's insinuation and not at all appeased by her
explanation, Ruth Dawson folded her arms
across her chest and took a firm stance. "And I'm
not in the habit, Miss Cathcart, of interfering
with things that are no business of mine." With a
"so there" bob of her head, Mrs. Dawson disappeared down the path.

"Oh, dear," sighed Margaret, "I really flubbed
that one! I think I've undone any good work I did
this morning!"

Switching the lights on, Margaret saw the object of her concern sitting on the little table
where she'd left it; the only difference was that,
instead of it being an unidentifiable paper-
wrapped parcel, it was now a delicately painted
doll, dressed in taffeta and lace.

Disbelievingly, Margaret searched under the
table and in the wastebaskets. Finally, in desperation, she looked in and around every exhibit.
Eventually positive the wrapping was nowhere
in the coach house, she turned off the lights and
locked the door.

Making her way up to the house, she pondered
the problem. Mrs. Dawson hadn't lied, she was
sure. There were many God-fearing women like
her, who thrived on local gossip, but whose lives
were ruled by the Ten Commandments. Still, ob-

viously someone had unwrapped the doll, so Mrs. Dawson must have been mistaken about no one else being there. Remembering her own entrance that morning, it would have been easy for a person to walk in unseen, particularly if Mrs. Dawson had been cleaning behind some of the larger exhibits. She shook her head. That wasn't clear thinking. It wasn't as if someone were walking in and right out again; it would take them time to unwrap the doll. Besides, in the quiet of the museum, Mrs. Dawson would be sure to hear the noise of the paper. So how had it been accomplished? And what about the woman she'd seen in the woods? No answers were forthcoming and she heaved a sigh. What she needed was a collaborator.

Coming out of her reverie, she saw Inspector Dobbs and his sergeant climbing the steps to the Hall. Quickening her stride, she rushed over to them. "Inspector, may I see you?"

The inspector turned. "I'm rather busy, at the moment, Miss Cathcart."

"I can appreciate that, Inspector, but I do have something important to tell you. It won't take long."

"I'm sure it will keep for a while, Miss Cathcart," said the inspector.

"But Inspector!" said Margaret.

For the first time, he took notice of her appearance. "Good Lord, Miss Cathcart," he exclaimed, "you haven't been attacked?"

"No, no," said Margaret aggravatedly. "I walked through the woods and—"

The inspector cut her off. "Well, then, I suggest, Miss Cathcart, you take a hot bath, have a strong cup of tea, and in the future, don't take such vigorous walks in the woods. You're a mess." He held the door for her, and as soon as all three were inside, strode off rapidly in the direction of the study.

Left standing, Margaret eyed his departing back with annoyance. He's impossible, she thought. Not only a grouch, but utterly impossible. Looking down at herself, however, she grudgingly agreed he was right about the bath; but that was as far as she would be intimidated. As for the tea... she'd have a brandy instead!

IN THE STUDY an hour later, Inspector Dobbs was reading through his latest reports. Of particular interest was the one that had come in on Marion Bundy's elusive husband, who had hurriedly left Kingscombe years earlier. The information proved both exciting and disappointing. Exciting because he'd worked for a chemical company in Canada up until four years ago. Disappointing because he'd dropped completely out of sight four years ago, and the Canadian authorities said he was no longer a resident of that country. They still planned to catch up with him, however. United States immigration had been contacted.

"Miss Cathcart insists on seeing you, sir," said Sergeant Buckingham, coming into the room. "She says it's very important." Noticing his superior's pained expression, he added, "Oh, she's all cleaned up now. Looks very presentable, and, if you don't mind my saying so, I think she did it for your benefit."

"Do you now, Bucks?" The inspector looked suddenly embarrassed and he grunted, "Good woman, that. Could be very attractive, too, if she gave it a try."

Sergeant Buckingham raised his eyebrows. His superior never ceased to surprise him.

"Here, read these," said the inspector, tossing a file folder across the desk. "See what you can make of them. The only one outside the norm is the vicar's."

The sergeant read the report on Richard Purdy first. "Hmm. . .I see what you mean. Got carried away, didn't he? Striking a fellow priest because he didn't agree with him."

"Nothing else on Mr. Bundy yet?" asked the sergeant, throwing the folder back on the desk. The inspector shook his head. "Should be more in soon. Meanwhile, the others are what you'd expect. Everyone's paid his taxes; two have had traffic tickets, none has a police record. . . ."

"Doesn't give us anything to go on."

"Not a damn thing."

"What about past connections? Those notes indicate a tie-up there."

The inspector shook his head in exasperation. "The only one left from that old wartime circle is Colonel Hawkins—unless you want to count Reverend Purdy and his sister, but they left when they were children."

"Do you think the colonel's life is in danger, then?" asked Buckingham.

"Frankly, I don't know. When I asked him about the figurine Miss Rochmere received, he didn't know anything about it. I'm not surprised. He was away at school for a good many years, and it *is* a little girl's toy. Nevertheless, he's the logical next victim. . .unless our murderer is going to stick to women. At any rate, I'm warning everyone again not to open packages, expected or otherwise, and to be extremely cautious."

"I don't think you'll have any trouble with
them following orders, sir," said the sergeant.

There was a discreet knock and Margaret entered, looking much more respectable than when
the inspector had seen her last.

"Come in, Miss Cathcart, come in. Sorry I was
so abrupt with you earlier. You said you had
something important?"

Margaret launched into her afternoon experience. When she had finished, the inspector
leaned back in his chair.

"You're sure it was Miss Twickham you saw?"
he asked.

Margaret thought for a minute. "I couldn't
swear to it. She was too far away for me to discern any features, but if someone asked me
whom I saw, I'd say Joyce Twickham."

"Let's see if we can find Miss Twickham now."
It took two telephone calls on the inspector's
part. While they were waiting for a reply to his
second, Inspector Dobbs used the time to full advantage to admonish Margaret for her rashness.

"You will not go wandering into the woods
again, Miss Cathcart, nor anywhere off the beat-
en track. Neither I nor my men have time to go
running off looking for foolhardy females who
don't have enough sense to use the brains God
gave them."

Margaret, sitting on the chair opposite, knew
he was absolutely right; but how dared he embarrass her this way in front of his sergeant! Her
anger and frustration were coming to a boiling
point. Fortunately for the inspector, the ringing
of the telephone cut off her retort.

His conversation was terse and to the point.
"Chief Inspector Dobbs here . . . you're posi-

tive...thank you...I appreciate what you've done." Replacing the receiver, he looked first at Sergeant Buckingham, then at Margaret.

"Miss Twickham arrived early this morning and is now at her sister's home. She expects to leave Tuesday."

"The police have actually seen her?" said Margaret.

The inspector nodded.

"Then who...?"

"Exactly, Miss Cathcart. Whom did you see in the woods today?"

8

MONDAY DAWNED another picture-book day with
bright sunshine and warm breezes, although
neither was appreciated by Inspector Dobbs until
the day was half over.

A good part of his frustrating morning was
taken up with studying a report that Marion
Bundy's husband was no longer a resident of the
United States and was now living in a South
American country, where it was hoped he would
be caught up with soon.

"Probably right in our front garden," said a
disgruntled Sergeant Buckingham.

"Do you think he's our murderer?" asked the
inspector.

"For my money, he's as likely a candidate as
we'll have." The sergeant began ticking off
reasons on his fingers: "A, he knew the two
deceased in the past; B, he has firsthand knowledge of chemical poisons; and C, from all reports,
he was the dashing, adventuresome kind, just
the type of person who might use an offbeat
poison for his murders."

"Perhaps you're right," said the inspector
thoughtfully. "But I wonder why he chose this
particular time to come up for air?"

He pondered the question for a moment, then
shook his head. "No, Bucks, it just doesn't jell . . .

and as far as that goes, neither does the ruined-garden business. In fact, I think we have two separate mysteries on our hands. And as much as I want to get our murderer behind bars, we've nothing really to go on until we find the parathion—and hope our man is lax in his own den—or catch up with Cecil Bundy. Other than the colonel, he's the only one left of that crowd that was here in January of 1942. I'm sure that year, when the blackmail started, is the key to this whole business. In the meantime," said the inspector, opening the door, "let's take another look at that damn wall of Miss Rochmere's. There has to be a way to get in."

After forty-five minutes of walking around and around, opening and closing the gate and peering up and over, they were as puzzled as ever. There was simply no way a person could climb over, or open the gate from the street side.

Inspector Dobbs heaved a sigh. "You know, sergeant, there are times when I wouldn't mind a taste of the nine-to-five routine. Why don't you take the car back to the Hall and check on any messages? Maybe they've finally located Bundy. I'm going to take a walk down by the water," he said, "in hopes the salt air will clear away the cobwebs."

Forty minutes later, Ronald Dobbs's romance with the sea was rudely interrupted by a familiar voice.

"Sergeant Buckingham said I'd find you here!" Margaret, draped in a loud, printed caftan, plunked herself down on the bench beside him. "Lovely day, isn't it? I've been looking for you all over the place. You are the hardest man to find, forever hopping from one place to another."

"It's difficult to solve a murder case from behind a desk," said the inspector dryly, looking out over the blue surface.

"And speaking of murderers," said Margaret, "are you any further ahead with our mysterious figure of yesterday?"

"Miss Cathcart," said the inspector, still not taking his gaze off the sea, "it is *my* mysterious figure, not ours. I spoke to Mrs. Dawson. She swears she didn't see anyone near the museum but you, and she never left it from the time she opened until she left. It was only after much prodding that we established there was a few minutes when she 'answered a call of nature.' This was just before she closed up."

"That's how they missed each other!" said Margaret.

"Exactly. And probably very fortunate for Mrs. Dawson," added the inspector.

"Well, we'll just have to figure it out," said Margaret firmly.

The inspector looked at her. "*We* will do no such thing," he stated. "For the last time, I shall ask you to stay out of it. I have no time to worry about amateurs bungling up a murder investigation." He rose from the bench. "And now, Miss Cathcart, if you'll excuse me, I must be getting back. I've spent far too much time in one place," he added caustically.

"Wait!" Margaret reached into her bag and took out a small jar. "Before you go, Inspector, I brought you this," she said, thrusting it into his unwary hand.

"What is it?"

"It's for your feet," she said smoothly. "I had it made up at the chemist's this morning."

Inspector Dobbs could feel his blood pressure rising, whether from embarrassment or anger, he wasn't sure. "What do you know about my feet?" he blustered.

"Now there's no need to be so embarrassed about it," said Margaret sweetly. "Sergeant Buckingham and I had a long talk," she added airily.

"The sergeant had no business—"

"Oh, don't be so churlish," she interrupted. "It's an old remedy given to my father. He had the same problem. The only thing you have to be careful of is to keep your shoes on when you use it. It smells something awful, but I guarantee it'll do the trick."

"Miss Cathcart," said the inspector, drawing himself up to his full height. "I assure you there is absolutely no need for you to look after my podiatric problem."

"Nonsense! I'm simply returning the consideration *you've* shown *me*—pointing out that I'm a mess and have the responsible mind of a three-year-old."

For a moment, watching the inspector's face, she wasn't sure if she was going to receive yet another blast. But suddenly the inspector threw back his head and guffawed.

"Miss Cathcart, you do get your barbs in! I stand duly chastised. But I still meant what I said," he added, his face losing all humor. "Don't get involved in this!"

"All right, I promise to be more careful. However, I do have a theory I'd like to discuss with you. It's—"

"Miss Margaret! I thought it was you, but the old eyes aren't so good any more, so I couldn't tell until I was up close."

Both of them turned to face an old man leaning heavily on a gnarled cane, his weather-beaten face creased into a profusion of wrinkles as he smiled a toothless welcome.

"Mr. Leavers! I haven't seen you in ages." Turning to the inspector, she explained, "When I was a little girl, I used to come down here and Mr. Leavers would tell me stories of all the brave sailors and their ships!" She looked back at the old mariner. "Remember how we'd sit out on the end of the old pier and you'd have me looking for mermaids?"

The old man chuckled. "Aye. It was the only way I could get you to be quiet long enough so I could tend to my fishing!"

"Are you still filling young minds with fantasy?" asked Margaret.

The old man shook his head sadly. "No, Miss Margaret, those days are gone forever. In this age of television and men going to the moon, children don't want to listen to folklore." He pointed toward the lopsided wharf. "Look, even the old pier has given up. Can't go out there anymore. The underpinnings are rotting away...."

Click! The film of an idea floated across Margaret's mind, but as quickly as it had come, it disappeared.

"...and the council has sealed up some of the caves. Said they were dangerous. People get lost in them or caught at high tide."

"Caves?" said the inspector.

The old man nodded and waved his cane toward the cliffs. "Aye. The cliffs are furrowed with them. This area used to be a regular pirates' paradise at one time. Like I said, most of the cave entrances on the beach here have been sealed shut, but all up and down the cliffs, where it's not so easy or likely children will go, there's still plenty of 'em left open."

The inspector had his own quickening thoughts as the old man rambled on. "Funny, how we never used to take precautions like that and the children had a whale of a time exploring them. Nowadays they think only of the consequences— look before you leap, that's the motto. Stilts the imagination, it does." For a few minutes the three of them discussed the old days, and then Margaret and the inspector began to make their way to the road.

"He's a rare breed, your Mr. Leavers. I like him. Not too many of them left anymore," said the inspector as he and Margaret walked up the cliff steps.

"He must be over ninety," said Margaret. "I know he had grandchildren when I was a child." She hesitated. "There was something he said back there . . . ."

"Yes?" queried the inspector.

"I . . . I don't know. Something seemed to register and then it was gone."

"To do with our murderer?"

Margaret shook her head. "I couldn't say, but it seems to me I should be brighter than I am today."

"What about this theory of yours?" asked the inspector when they reached the top.

"Oh, yes. The theory, well, I got to thinking—"

"Inspector!"

Sergeant Buckingham squealed the car to a stop and left the engine running. "That report you wanted, sir, about Mrs. Bundy's husband. Central called and you're to ring them right back. I believe they've found him, sir."

Inspector Dobbs wasted no time on goodbyes, hasty or otherwise. Jumping into the car, he shouted to "get on with it," leaving Margaret in a swirl of silk caftan as the sergeant sped away.

"Murder investigation or no, I swear I'm going to teach that man some manners!" she said aloud, smoothing her dress. "Didn't even offer me a ride!"

She was still fuming when she met almost head-on with Emily on the High Street.

"Emily!"

The sharpness of Margaret's voice brought the girl up short.

"Miss Cathcart! I'm sorry. I didn't see you."

"Emily! Where on earth are you going, child?" She paused, then asked, "Did you enjoy your day yesterday?"

"Oh, Miss Cathcart! Am I glad to see you! Yesterday was terrible! John and I are like strangers! I. . . I just don't know what to do! I'm at my wit's end!" To Emily's mortification, tears welled up in her eyes. "I can't explain half of what's going on. I had a terrifying nightmare, I'm hearing voices in the night, seeing things I don't understand. . . . I think I'm losing my mind!"

Margaret took the young girl's hand and squeezed it in her generous palm while at the same time seeking a refuge for the obviously distressed Emily. Tucking the younger woman's arm protectively into her side, she began to cross the road. "Come on. We'll have some tea and you can tell me all about it."

"I can't," wailed Emily, now making no pretense to hide the tears. "I have to get back to the shop. I've already had an hour's lunch and. . .

and we're doing a boom...boom...booming business. You know, curiosity seekers."

"The shop can wait," said Margaret firmly. "You're going to pour forth your troubles to Aunty Margaret and the devil can take care of the Bell."

There was only one other table occupied in the tea shop. Three middle-aged women sat there, reliving with great relish their visit to the Bell. "My dear! Do you realize we actually stood on the spot where that poor woman was murdered?"

"It gives one a sense of being part of history...."

With concentrated effort, Margaret switched them off and turned her attention to Emily. She knew better than to ply the girl with questions, so she waited patiently till Emily had finished almost two cups of tea and started her story of her own volition. She talked about Friday's nightmare, Sarah's odd remark on Saturday evening, the argument she'd overheard between John and his aunt and their obvious coverup.

Margaret let Emily ramble on until the latter got it all out of her system, and when the young woman finally did stop, Margaret's voice was firm. "There are explanations for all of these," she said. "We have only to find them."

"That's easy to say but difficult to do," said Emily despondently, dabbing at her red-rimmed eyes. "I wouldn't know where to start."

"The obvious place is with Sarah Loft. What did she say about Friday night, by the way?"

Emily shrugged. "That it was a nightmare and nothing more. Perhaps she's right," said Emily quietly.

"She never mentioned the argument you over-heard?"

"No," said Emily.

". . . I went to an auction last Thursday . . . some lovely things. . . ." That strident voice at the next table kept filtering through Margaret's concentration. She forced herself back to Emily's problems.

"Neither did John," Emily was saying, "but it was some argument and he went off in a huff. Yet yesterday morning they both acted as sweet-ly to each other as they'd ever done."

"Again, you never brought the subject up?"

"No. I didn't want to rock the boat."

"Emily, you can't act wishy-washy in these things. You have to take a firm stance. Now fin-ish your tea while I pay the bill. Then I'm going to have a talk with Sarah Loft . . . whether she's in-viting guests or not. And then I'm—"

". . . and those Queen Anne legs!" said the lady at the next table. "So fragile-looking. . . ."

Click! The sudden look of surprised astonish-ment on Margaret's face caused Emily some con-cern.

"Miss Cathcart?" she said tentatively.

Margaret hastily pushed back her chair. "I must rush," she said. "I've just remembered something that's been bothering me for the past two days." She patted a startled Emily's hand. "Don't worry, now, everything's going to be fine. You go back to the shop and don't fret. But don't go back to Rose Hill until you hear from me . . . or the inspector!" she called back from the doorway.

She was out of the door before Emily could gather her thoughts.

Reaching the Hall in record time, Margaret headed straight for the study, knocked once, and without waiting for a reply, pulled open the door.

"Inspector, I . . . ."

"He's not here, Miss Cathcart," said Sergeant Buckingham, getting up from the chair behind the desk. "I expect him back within an hour. Perhaps I. . . ."

But Margaret didn't wait. Whirling around she headed back for the front door and outside. Fifteen minutes later she was leaning on a front doorbell, determined someone inside should answer. After two minutes of persistent ringing, the door was yanked open.

"I should have guessed," said a gruff voice.

Margaret's jaw dropped. "Inspector! What are you doing here?"

"Doesn't it strike you that I should be asking that question? Miss Cathcart, *you are meddling again!*"

"No, I'm not!" said Margaret. "If you'd stay at your headquarters sometimes, things like this wouldn't happen! I tried to find you! You see, a woman at the next table in the tea shop made me remember. She was talking about Queen Anne furniture, how frail and delicate it looks, and it struck me all of a sudden—what had been bothering me ever since Saturday night in the library. Sarah Loft's legs didn't go with her body!"

Much to her surprise, the inspector didn't bat an eye. He simply opened the door invitingly. "You'd better come in," he said.

Margaret fidgeted in the hall while Inspector Dobbs went into a room at the left and closed the door. A short while later he came back, a scowl on his face. "We've decided to take you into our confidence," he said. "I can't say as I like the idea, but you will persist in butting into other people's affairs! What you are about to see and hear is to be held in the strictest secrecy, and if you so much as breathe a word, I shall cut out your tongue. Is that understood?"

Margaret nodded a silent agreement.

"Then come with me, and for heaven's sake be quiet!" he said, leading her into the room from which he'd just come.

The heavy draperies were drawn, and the only light came from a powerful lamp set up on a small table. Two men, John Trask and another she'd never seen, were studying a wrinkled piece of paper spread out before them and diligently writing in little notebooks.

Softly, the inspector closed the door. Peering about the room, Margaret saw something that made her smother a scream and involuntarily grope for the inspector's arm. It was the dress Sarah had worn the previous day when they were in the garden. It was on the bed, not lying there but sitting up and looking exactly as it did when Sarah Loft was wearing it...except that no head protruded above the neckline. The inspector was elated with Margaret's reaction.

"Gives you a jolt, doesn't it?" he whispered. For the second time, Margaret nodded in silent agreement, unable for a moment to pull her gaze from the stuffed dress.

Letting her eye move to the dressing table, she made out another part of Sarah Loft—gray hair mounted on a wigstand.

Margaret looked up at the inspector and opened her mouth, but he stifled anything she had to say by putting a finger to his lips. Motioning her toward the settee, they sat without speaking.

The heavy silence was finally broken by the door being opened. A tall, thin woman entered the room and crossed to the men. At first glance, Margaret thought it was Joyce Twickham—by this time, nothing would have surprised her—but quickly she realized that the features and gestures were entirely wrong.

"Had any luck breaking the code?" said the woman.

"Not yet," said John Trask.

"You will," said the woman, patting his shoulder. "Keep the faith."

The woman approached Margaret and the inspector. "Miss Cathcart," she said, smiling with outstretched hand. "My sincere congratulations. I wondered if you would spot the discrepancy last Saturday, because not for a moment did I underestimate your intelligence. I just thank God you have sense enough to go to the authorities with your story and no one else."

Margaret took the hand and looked into the familiar brown eyes. "Sarah Loft!" she exclaimed. "What on earth is going on around here?"

Sarah gave a brief smile. "It's a rather complicated situation, but under the circumstances I think you're entitled to an explanation." She pulled up a small chair and sat down. "To begin with, John and I are here on an assignment, one we hope will be finished within the next few days."

"Assignment?" said Margaret blankly.

Sarah nodded. "You see, we both work for Interpol. . .in the Diamond Security Branch."

"Diamonds!" exclaimed Margaret.

"Ssh . . ." commanded the inspector.

Sarah glanced at the two men working under the lamp. "I think, perhaps, I'd better send John for Emily. I could see how upset she was this morning, and since now seems to be the time for explanations, she should be in on them."

"She's at the Bell," said Margaret, "and she's very confused and frightened—even of John. She mentioned a quarrel you and your nephew had the other night."

"Oh, dear," said Sarah.

"I'd better call Sergeant Buckingham to go over," said Ronald Dobbs. He began to dial on the telephone that sat on the small table by his elbow.

"Good," said Sarah. "John will follow and bring her back here. He can tell her a few basics on the way." She got up and crossed to the two men, spoke a few words to John, who nodded and headed for the door. Sarah turned and motioned Margaret and the inspector to follow her. "It's homier in the kitchen," she said.

When the three of them were comfortably seated around the table, glasses of sherry before them, Sarah resumed her story.

"Remember, now, Margaret," she warned, "what I'm about to tell you must be kept in the utmost secrecy. We've worked too hard and too long to have our cover blown now."

"Of course," said Margaret. "I already understand that, but what on earth does Kingscombe have to do with diamonds?"

As serious as the situation was, Sarah allowed herself a smile. "I don't blame you for being knocked for a loop," she said, "and I'll try to make my explanation as precise and clear as possible. A few months ago, we received a tip that a large packet of stolen diamonds was coming through Kingscombe. The informant gave us the name of the person receiving them, the fact that they were brought in by sea, and that they were to be exchanged for money during the D.M.O.'s sight in London, to be held during the first week of May.''

"D.M.O.'s sight?'' repeated Margaret.

Sarah shook her head in self-annoyance. "I'm sorry,'' she said, "of course you wouldn't know what I was talking about. First of all, let me explain that the diamond industry is very tightly controlled and closed-circuited. Each year, based on supply and demand, the diamond industry cartel releases only so many dollars' worth of stones on the market, and this supply has to be divided among the world's dealers. Now, several times a year, the Diamond Marketing Organization—D.M.O.—holds sights, where dealers are invited to buy parcels of diamonds. These parcels, again, are heavily controlled by the cartel, inasmuch as a dealer must accept the parcel he is offered, without inspecting the stones; he won't get another chance to buy until the next sight.''

"It doesn't seem very fair,'' said Margaret.

Sarah shrugged. "It has its good points. If diamonds weren't tightly controlled, they'd be as common as rhinestones. Of course,'' she added sardonically, "it also has its drawbacks. As with anything in great demand, it breeds its own corruption. I don't think there is any other mineral that causes more evildoing than diamonds—men steal, even kill for them. Our problem is we can't touch the real organizers of diamond thefts and

smuggling because they are—they must be—
members of the strong, elite clique of the diamond industry itself. They are the only people in
the position to lay their hands on diamonds that
are not on the open market! So we in the Diamond Security Branch never hope to catch the
big fish, but if we can hook the small fish, the
hired, professional couriers, the illicit buyers
themselves and, of course, the diamonds, then
we feel we're at least undermining the organization a little."

Sarah sighed and went on, "And like most of
the public, Margaret, you have no idea how often
history has been changed, and will still be
changed, by these little gems. Wherever there's a
hotbed of revolt, you can bet your bottom dollar
illicit diamonds have been in there somewhere."

"You mean these diamonds that are coming into Kingcombe might end up paying for guns and
ammunition?"

"A good chance, yes," said Sarah. "Believe
me, our branch keeps a close eye on known revolutionaries and mercenaries."

"Are there revolutionaries here, in Kingscombe?" said Margaret, aghast.

Sarah allowed herself another smile at Margaret's incredulity. "No, not that we know of,"
she said. "A courier is here, however."

"Who?" asked Margaret.

"George Knight."

"George! I don't believe it! He wouldn't do
anything like that!"

"Oh yes, he would...and does," said Sarah.
"He's a very greedy man, our George Knight, and
that's been his undoing. It was his greed, in fact,
that cut out our informant from this sweet little

deal, so the worm turned on him. Actually, George Knight is lucky to be still walking around. As I said, this is a cutthroat game.''

"Good Lord!" exclaimed Margaret.

"Yes, good Lord, exactly," said Sarah. "Unfortunately, time is running out on us, and we don't seem to be making too much headway." She paused, taking a sip of her sherry. "Did you see that piece of paper John and the other man were poring over?"

Margaret nodded.

"Well, somewhere in the figures written on it, there's a code that tells us where and when George is supposed to dispose of the diamonds in London. By the way," she added, "you were the one who helped us on that!"

"Me?" said Margaret. "What did I do?"

"You gave us the connection we've been waiting for, simply by a chance remark you made while sitting in my garden yesterday."

"I did?" said Margaret.

Again Sarah nodded. "Our informant told us that the diamonds were coming by ship to a George Knight in Kingscombe and were to be exchanged in London the first week of May. But there was one other thing. George was to receive a coded message telling him exactly where and when the exchange was to take place, and it was with this information that I came to Kingscombe, with two objectives: to find the diamonds and learn where and when the exchange was to be made."

Margaret frowned. "But your disguise. . . ?"

"A newcomer to such a small place as Kingscombe might have aroused George Knight's suspicions—he might have guessed he was being watched. We wanted him to feel absolutely secure in the belief that no one knew of his illegal doings. That's why we decided to establish my identity as someone who couldn't get around easily and wanted privacy—he'd never feel suspicious of such a person."

"But it's such a transformation!"

"Actually, it wasn't too difficult," said Sarah. "Padded gowns and a wig did most of it. The only part we were really concerned about was my hands. Instead of trying to hide them, I gave them the illusion of fatness by wearing large rings that squeezed into the flesh. They alone made my hands look puffy."

Margaret was amazed. "How on earth could you stand them on all the time?"

"You forget. There were very few hours of the day I was with anyone. In the mornings I'd be up when Emily and Mrs. Dawson were around, then I'd retire to my room to 'write.' Mrs. Dawson always left my lunch on a tray, so there was no reason for me to emerge until suppertime . . . and no one could ever call me a night owl!"

"But what 'connection' did I give you?" asked Margaret eagerly.

"For weeks, now," said Sarah, "we've watched the antique shop, even planted Emily there—"

Margaret gasped.

"Yes, I'm afraid we used her, but I'll tell you more about that later. Anyway, for some time we had no luck in hearing or seeing anything untoward happening. Then, yesterday, something unusual did happen. George Knight came looking for Emily. Now why, I asked myself, should he come looking for her on a Sunday? And why should he get so upset when he found she wasn't home and couldn't be reached because she was out for a day's drive? I tell you, he was fit to be tied. He was so frantic, in fact, that he tipped his hand...or so I thought. You see, he asked if Emily had brought anything here from the shop on Saturday. I didn't want him to know that I knew she and John had stopped in Saturday night to pick up the doll that needed mending, so I said no, knowing full well that the object in question was probably, by then, somewhere at the Hall, and also knowing that sooner or later, George'd probably come to the conclusion that, since it wasn't at the shop or here, Emily had dropped it off at the museum. That's why I was keeping him here—in hopes I could think of some way to get to the museum before he did. And then *you* came along and mentioned the parcel Emily had given you, and that you'd left it at the museum. And the first thing he asked was if the doll was wrapped for protection. That's when I realized it wasn't the doll he was after but the paper Emily had wrapped it in. I can't tell you how relieved I was when you told me he was put in hospital, because up until then, I honestly didn't know how I was going to get it before he did."

"You were the woman I saw running from the museum!"

"Yes," said Sarah, "the inspector told me about that, and Emily told me the vicar's sister thought she saw Miss Twickham on the pier in the wee hours of Saturday morning. I must admit I wasn't very discreet when out of disguise, but then, I didn't expect anyone in the village to be looking out their window at three a.m., nor you sitting in the woods on your cousin's estate Sunday afternoon.''

The man who'd been studying the sheet of paper with John Trask came into the kitchen. ''I'm taking this into headquarters,'' he said. ''I can't crack it, but it shouldn't take the experts too long. I'll be in touch as soon as I have something,'' he said, then disappeared down the hall.

For the next minute, everyone was lost in his own thoughts, then Margaret frowned. ''What did you mean . . . that you used Emily?''

''Ah, yes,'' said Sarah. ''I do feel somewhat badly about that. But I can't deny that most of my guilt feelings disappear when I see her and John together,'' she added in a softer tone.

Margaret's frown deepened. ''But how did she get mixed up in this?''

''I'm afraid,'' said Sarah, ''that it happened to be a case of us taking advantage of her situation: her knowledge of antiques and the fact that she wanted to get away. You see, one of our people who's employed in the mineralogy department of the museum where Emily works in Canada, overheard her telling friends of her desire to get away from it all. He approached her with the idea that she come to England and stay with me—a semi-invalid who needed a secretary-companion. We made it so attractive for her, she couldn't refuse.''

''But why?'' said Margaret.

''We needed someone to be our eyes and ears inside the shop, even though that someone wasn't aware of anything going on. I gave Emily plenty of free time to gravitate naturally to the Bell, and once her interest was aroused, it was simply a matter of suggesting to your cousin that

George Knight would be the man to attend to the toy-museum displays and that my newfound secretary could mind the shop.''

"So you used Charles, too!''

Sarah didn't turn a hair at the accusation. "I'm sure the inspector can tell you that, in our line of work, we must use any means at our disposal,'' she said.

Margaret turned toward Ronald Dobbs, who'd been quietly sitting back, smoking his pipe and sipping his sherry, throughout Sarah's explanation. "And what have you to do with this?'' she asked.

"Not a thing,'' he assured her complacently. "In fact, I knew nothing about any diamond business until a short while ago, when Mrs. Loft asked me to come here.''

"When John and I came to Kingscombe,'' said Sarah, "we hadn't intended to get in touch with the police; we usually don't. The second murder, however, changed all that. At first, we weren't sure if Alicia Rochmere's death was somehow connected with the diamond smuggling. We admit poison was an unorthodox method, but as I stated before, killing is not new to these people.''

"You suspected Alicia was connected with the diamond smuggling?'' said Margaret. "But that's ridiculous! She's the last person who'd do wrong!''

The inspector wondered what she would say if he told her then and there that her sweet little lady was a blackmailer. He reminded himself that when this case was cleared up, he must educate Miss Cathcart as to the ways of criminals.

"So we decided to sit back and see what would happen,'' Sarah went on. "But then, when

Marion Bundy was poisoned, it was a little too much to accept, even in the diamond-smuggling business, so we thought we'd better contact the inspector.''

''You mean there's no connection between the murders and the smuggling?''

''None, as far as we're concerned,'' said Sarah.

''I agree,'' said the inspector. ''The murders are *my* problem,'' he added with a significant look at Margaret, who chose to ignore it.

Instead, she turned toward Sarah. ''But the diamonds,'' she said, ''where are they?''

''That's just it,'' said Sarah. ''We know where they *should* be, but we haven't been able to find them. We're hoping perhaps Emily can help us.''

As if on cue, the front door banged shut, and an exhilarated Emily and John came into the kitchen.

''She knows most of the story,'' said John. ''I'll let you fill her in on some of the other details.''

While Emily recovered from her initial shock at seeing Sarah ''in the flesh,'' and John and the inspector filled her in on other happenings, Margaret and Sarah busied themselves preparing sandwiches and coffee. Finally, when the table was set, they sat down and joined the rest.

''I can't get over it!'' exclaimed Emily, looking at her hostess. ''I can't believe you're the same person!''

''Well, I am, my dear,'' said Sarah, patting the young woman's hand, ''and I have several apologies to make to you.'' She sat back in her chair. ''I suppose I should begin with Friday night. You see, I had arranged to meet Interpol's man on the pier—he was an officer on the ship we believe brought in the diamonds to George, and because I didn't expect to be seen I didn't bother with the 'heavy' me.''

"It was you Miss Purdy saw on the pier, then, not Miss Twickham!" said Emily. "It's not difficult to see how she could make the mistake. You're built the same way.''

"So I have found out," said Sarah dryly. "Anyway, Emily, my dear, I couldn't risk your hearing or seeing me, so I slipped a sedative into your saucepan of milk while it was heating—you'd turned your back for a moment. Unfortunately, as we soon learned, the drug had an undesirable effect on you, and rather than making you sleep heavily, it succeeded only in putting you into a paralyzed dream state.''

"The motorboat . . . the water . . ." said Emily.

"The man I met used a motor launch," said Sarah. "I came back in, rinsed out your thermos and glass, then swilled regular milk in them. It was then I made the mistake of closing your door." Sarah took a bite of her sandwich.

"The quarrel Emily mentioned between you and John . . ." prompted Margaret.

"When it comes to you, Emily, John is not at all rational. He was very angry that I'd drugged your milk.''

John reached for Emily's hand.

"I hope it won't take them too long to break that code," said Sarah, looking at the clock.

"This paper, with the code on it," said Margaret. "Where did it come from?''

Sarah looked surprised. "The Nottinghams, of course! George Knight's Saturday cake order was wrapped up in it. You see, the Nottinghams were intermediaries for the couriers. Although we've not approached them yet, I'm pretty sure we'll find they didn't know what was going on and were only doing this for a fee."

"Did George read it?" asked Margaret.

"What if your office doesn't crack the code?" chimed in Emily.

"In answer to your question, Margaret, no, I don't think he had time to read it. That's why he was so frantic about its whereabouts. Whether they crack the code or not, Emily, our action will be the same. If George Knight is still in hospital at the beginning of the week, we'll arrange for his release, so he can pick up the paper, which we'll put back on the doll."

"Then it really doesn't matter if your office doesn't break the code," said Margaret. "You could still have George followed."

"We will," said Sarah, "but it's tricky. Contraband *usually* changes hands in a bustling public place, which means George Knight could wander around London for two or three days and pass the diamonds anytime." She turned her attention to Emily. "And speaking of diamonds, we need your help. There was a wooden crate delivered to the Bell on Saturday morning. We know the diamonds are concealed somewhere in that shipment, but we can't find them! The man I met on the pier had examined the contents and crate thoroughly and couldn't come up with a clue. There are no hollowed-out boards, no splits, no false tops, sides or bottoms in the crate itself. He wasn't, however, too sure of the antique itself, not being an expert in that field. That's why we want you to examine it."

"Oh, but I can't," Emily wailed. "Mr. Knight uncrated it yesterday, and the buyer picked it up this morning!"

Her statement sent a shock wave across the room. "But we need it!" said Sarah.

"Wait!" At John Trask's authoritative command, four pairs of eyes swung his way. "George Knight wouldn't have let that antique go if it contained the diamonds, so obviously, he's either removed them from the antique or they are still in the crate somewhere."

"Oh, dear," said Emily miserably, "that's gone, too. It was all broken up and thrown out when I opened the shop this morning!"

"That means George has removed the diamonds and stashed them someplace in his home or shop," said John.

"Which means we have to get a search warrant in a hurry," said Sarah. "Thank heavens he's in the hospital."

During this brief conversation, Emily had been sitting quietly, remembering something she'd seen that morning. She'd thought nothing of it at the time, but... "I don't know if this means anything," she said, "but today, when I went into the desk, I saw he'd kept the bolts that had secured the corners of the box . . . but then again, he keeps all sorts of odds and ends."

Sarah and John weren't paying attention to her last statement. Sarah was the first out of her seat. "That's it, John. The bolts!" They raced for the car.

It was very late when the inspector drove Margaret back to the Hall. Everything had gone well at the Bell. Most of the diamonds had been removed from the hollowed-out bolts—a few were left in order to make the arrest legal—and the tiny cavities filled with glass to achieve the previous weight. What was more, Interpol had broken the code and knew where the exchange was to take place. George Knight would be released from the hospital at the last possible moment, with just enough time to pick up the paper and the bolts, but no time to examine the diamonds.

Ronald Dobbs looked over at his companion. She really had been quite pleasant to have around, he thought. Granted, she sometimes babbled on about inconsequential things, such as, was Sarah's name her real one, was John her nephew, and was she actually a writer. The answers were yes to the first two, and a reserved "not up until now" to the last. It had been a most satisfying night. "Now that we have one mystery solved," he said, "what about this theory you mentioned on the beach today? You never did get a chance to explain it."

But one mystery was Margaret's quota for the day. She yawned loudly. "Later," she mumbled. "I think we've all had enough for one day."

9

THE FOLLOWING DAY, Tuesday, while Marion
Bundy remained on a slab pending the wishes of
her malingering husband, Alicia Rochmere was
laid to rest in the weed-choked churchyard.

Inspector Dobbs, standing unobtrusively by the
open grave, wondered about the dead woman's
will. Alicia had left her money to the vicar, but
to whom had that £23,000 rightfully belonged?
The woman who had it in her bank account, or
the woman who paid it out? With both parties
dead, it was pure conjecture. He sighed. Well, it
wasn't his problem. Let the legal minds argue it
in court. He had a murderer to outwit.

He looked around at the funeral assemblage.
As was expected, most of the village had turned
out; not only was Alicia Rochmere a longtime
resident, but she was a murder victim, and
violent death had a strange attraction for the living. He studied the faces of those standing nearby. Colonel Hawkins and the Cathcart sisters
were standing together. Both Sarah and John
Trask were in London, but Emily King was there,
huddled in the protective arm of Margaret
Cathcart. Amy Purdy stood to the right of this
tightly knit group, and on its left was the colonel's chauffeur, Franks.

The inspector's eyes scanned the others. The

whole Dawson clan was there, including Grace, who kept looking at Franks with a doe-eyed expression. From what the inspector could see, however, the young man acknowledged Grace with only a brief smile.

He continued studying the faces—mostly blank facades—staring at the casket. A few showed some emotion, and now and again a tissue or handkerchief was produced to wipe away a tear as the Reverend Richard Purdy droned on.

"Dust to dust, ashes to ashes." The vicar was winding up the service.

Reaching into his pocket, the inspector took out a note and read it for a second time. Cecil Bundy, Marion Bundy's roving husband, had been found in Brazil and was arriving at Heathrow Airport in London that morning. Turning his back on the others, he briskly walked through the stubble and grass to his own car, which a young constable quickly brought to life. Getting in, the inspector commented, "I've paid my respects. Now let's go on to London, so I can talk to Mr. Bundy."

Three times during the afternoon and evening, Margaret knocked on the study door, ready to relay her theory, only to be told by a busy Sergeant Buckingham that the inspector had not yet come back. It was well past midnight when Ronald Dobbs did return, whereupon he had a long conference with the sergeant. While the two men talked, the search for the parathion went on.

During the daylight hours of Tuesday, the police had ceased scaling the cliffs for fear of further alarming the already frightened villagers, or worse, possibly panicking their murderer if he

suspected they were getting close to his hoard.
The cliffs, however, had been constantly kept
under surveillance by men in boats. And finally,
early Wednesday morning, their efforts were
rewarded. The five-gallon drum of parathion was
found buried in an abandoned cave, accessible
only by a precipitous path from the top of a cliff,
its narrow opening well protected by crag and
brush. The murderer was just as meticulous here
as he had been with the packages—no clue to his
identity had been left. Any equipment he had
needed to protect himself from the poison or to
prepare his lethal gifts had been removed—and
not in haste. Even the floor had been carefully
twig-brushed to obliterate any incriminating
footprints. He was a most careful man.

"Thank God he was," said the inspector,
standing above as the drum of parathion was removed carefully from its hiding place. "Can you
imagine what could have happened if he'd
slipped or fallen with that stuff in his hands?"

None of the men watching the maneuvers
needed to comment.

KINGSCOMBE EXPERIENCED its next tragedy
Wednesday morning. The weather was turning
foul. Cold winds blew in off the sea, bringing
threatening clouds with them. Emily, on her way
to the post office, instinctively snuggled her chin
into her coat. Most people unused to English
dampness would be chilled to the bone, but Emily had her own inner fire to keep her warm. She
had accepted John's proposal of marriage.

She hurried into the protection of the post office entranceway and pushed against the door. It
was locked. Emily rattled the knob. Miss Twick-

ham always opened at eight, and here it was twenty minutes past and the door was locked. The postmistress was in there, though. Peering through the glass, Emily could see her sitting on the stool behind the counter, a welcoming smile on her homely face. Emily banged on the glass. Why on earth didn't she answer? She was looking directly at her. Emily cupped her hands around her face for a better view, and cold terror replaced exhilaration. Miss Twickham's expression wasn't a smile of welcome, but a grimace of death. The long, lavender hat pin Emily had admired a few days earlier was protruding from Miss Twickham's skull, just above and to the front of the right ear.

"DEATH WAS INSTANTEOUS, due to penetration of the brain. Couldn't have been more than an hour ago.

"She was taken by surprise. No evidence of struggle." These were the words of the medical examiner to Inspector Dobbs.

"Anyone see anything?" the inspector asked a rain-soaked Sergeant Buckingham when he came in from questioning the nearby shopkeepers.

"Not a thing, sir. That doesn't mean, of course, the murderer couldn't have been under their noses. Since most of them don't open till eight-thirty or nine, they were busy stocking shelves or doing book work, not paying attention to the passersby."

The inspector sighed in resignation. "I don't suppose our murderer was foolish enough to take a chance on walking out the front door anyway, Bucks. Why is it when we want our man to be seen, he never is, but when Mrs. Loft didn't want

anyone to see her, two people were in the most
unlikely places at the most unlikely times. Sometimes I'm inclined to agree with the vicar; the
devil does rear his ugly head."

"Don't be discouraged, sir," said the sergeant
encouragingly. "He'll make his mistake."

"He already has," said the inspector gravely.
"He's panicked."

"Sir?" said the sergeant.

"The other two were planned murders, Bucks.
This one wasn't. If Miss Twickham was on his
list, she would have died by the same method.
That makes it easier for us because now we have
a new piece in the puzzle. Somehow, Bucks,
Joyce Twickham became a threat to him *after*
the first two murders."

The sergeant frowned. "I can't entirely agree,
sir," said the sergeant. "Even though we found
the parathion last night, it doesn't necessarily
follow that he didn't intend eventually to kill her
in the usual way."

"Oh, but it does," insisted the inspector.
"Remember, our man made elaborate prepara-
tions; he knew his victims well. But when we
found the drum, there was every indication that
he was finished with it; or, God forbid, he's
already prepared a package for another victim. I
seriously doubt if our murderer knows, or even
cares, that we've found his supply. If he'd had a
surprise package prepared for Miss Twickham,
he would have used it instead of the pin."

Both men saw him at the same time. A man
stood at the door, water dripping from his shiny
raincoat and peaked cap. It was the sergeant who
realized that the wetness on the man's face was
from tears, not rain, and he walked over to him.

"Mr. Jenkins, isn't it, sir?" he said. "Mr. Seth Jenkins, the postman?"

"Where is she?"

Sergeant Buckingham blocked any further entry. "I'm afraid, sir, you can't see her. Are you a relative?"

"We were going to be married," said the man.

"Mr. Jenkins," said the inspector quietly, "let's sit in the car for a few minutes. I'd like to ask you a few questions."

It took a little time to get Mr. Jenkins to focus his mind on previous events, but finally, they succeeded in draining his story out.

Miss Twickham had arrived on the nine-twenty train out of London last night and had been in very good spirits. He'd met her at the station, and together they'd walked the short distance to the post office, where she'd made them a cup of tea. They'd talked about her trip and the murders in Kingscombe until he had left around eleven. No, she hadn't been nervous or excited or upset. She'd told him about the wedding and said that her journey there and back had been uneventful.

"Miss Twickham didn't say, perhaps, that she had any surprises?"

"Surprises, Inspector? I don't know what you mean...."

"I mean.... No, forget it, Mr. Jenkins." The inspector sighed. "I don't mean anything."

The postman reached for the door handle. "If you're through with me, I'd like to leave."

"Of course...but why not stay in the car? Sergeant Buckingham and I have to be going back in the shop, but Constable Reed will drive you home."

The crime photographer and lab team had just about finished when P.C. Reed returned after dropping off Mr. Jenkins. Hurrying over to the inspector, he handed him a note.

"Stopped off at the police station, sir, and this message was phoned in about an hour ago."

The inspector looked at the paper. A Mrs. Thompson on Priory Road had reported that all her flowers had been ruined beyond salvation. What made it so incomprehensible to her was that her garden was inaccessible from the outside!

They stopped at the Priory Road address on the way back to the Hall. It was just as Mrs. Thompson had said, no one could get into the garden without going through the house. The garden was surrounded by a seven-foot wall, on top of which was a two-foot-high, densely thick, thorny hedge. The gate was a narrow, plain, flat wooden one, but too high to vault. A wishing-well-type roof hung over it at such a steep pitch that the top of the tall gate missed it only by inches. The latch, they noticed, was similar to the one at Alicia Rochmere's garden and could only be opened from the garden side.

"You know, sir," said Sergeant Buckingham, in a suddenly talkative mood, "I have to admit that I wasn't entirely sold on your idea that a ladder couldn't have been used at the Rochmere place. I mean, even after you explained about the chances one would take being seen and all, and having to be extremely careful of the shards of glass. . . . But now this one, with that thorn bush on top, does look impossible to climb over, and there's no way I can see anyone scaling that steep roof over the gate—not in the short time he'd probably have before someone came along." The sergeant sighed deeply. The problem was really very complex. "And then, of course, there's still the matter as to what to do with the ladder, even if one does have an accomplice...." He heaved another heavy sigh, his voice dwindling away as other mental options took form. During the short drive back to the Hall, Sergeant Buckingham sighed a great deal, while his superior inwardly fumed.

Upon entering the study, the inspector irritably banged the door. "Damn it, Bucks, we're being played for fools! When I get my hands on the culprit...."

THE POLICE IN WALTHAM DALE had promised to retrace Miss Twickham's steps and call back. Meanwhile, Inspector Dobbs and Sergeant Buckingham again went over the list of people who were at the party Saturday night.

"We can eliminate Sarah Loft, John Trask and Emily King."

"Also our prime candidate," sighed the sergeant, "Marion Bundy's husband. Thank God. Now she can be buried."

"At least when I was talking with him in London yesterday, he cleared up the mystery as to why Marion died a virgin," said the inspector.

Sergeant Buckingham shook his head in disbelief. "I still can't comprehend it. Marriage of convenience! I thought that went out with hoop skirts and crinolines."

"People will do many things for money, Bucks."

"Oh, I don't blame either of them, sir. It's the old man I'm thinking of. Imagine forcing your only daughter to marry the son of your girl friend for the sole purpose of having a grandson by him!''

The inspector threw down his pen. ''Marion wasn't stupid. She knew she couldn't fight her father or he'd cut her off without a penny, so she demurely went through the marriage, then told Cecil she'd have nothing to do with him. It suited them both. He'd always had a roving eye, and as long as he kept his affairs discreet, he had Marion's blessing. They both worked hard to keep the controller of the purse strings satisfied that all was well in the bed chamber, and if nature didn't see fit to produce a grandchild, there was nothing they could do about it. Outwardly they were a loving couple. Then one day the inevitable happened. Cecil fell in love with one of his conquests.''

''The barmaid.''

''Right. To give Marion Bundy her due, she knew of Cecil's plight and gave him an out—£5,000 to disappear. It gave them both an out, actually. That way, all the blame fell on Cecil—no wonder he didn't want to come back here—and Marion played the part of the jilted woman to the hilt. She even went away to 'recuperate from a broken heart.' Her father, by this time, was quite old, and whether he believed her story or not, he left her as sole heir when he died in 1961.''

As though in common consent, the two men sat silently, their features relaxed as each contemplated the strange affairs at Redwing almost twenty years earlier. Then slowly, the relaxed attitude left the inspector's face and a look of enlightenment took over. With a loud smack, his palm struck the desk top. ''Good God, that's it!''

he thundered. "Marion Bundy's father died in
1961—the year the payments to Miss Rochmere
stopped! There's the connection, Bucks." Impatiently, he scattered papers on the desk.
"Where's that damn bankbook?"

Sergeant Buckingham quickly extracted it from
a file folder. "Here, sir."

Rapidly, the inspector turned the pages of the
book, and ran a finger down the last page of en-
tries. "Yes. Yes, here it is. June 10, 1961, one
hundred pounds. The last payment! Let's get a
confirmation of the death date." He picked up
the phone and dialed. "It'll be in the church
records."

When at last Inspector Dobbs hung up the
phone, he heaved a sigh, and then a broad smile
crossed his face. "Well, it isn't easy talking to the
reverend, Bucks, but at least this time it paid
off." His eyes flashed with excitement. "July 5,
1961. When Marion Bundy's father died, the payments stopped."

The sergeant's face creased into a puzzled
frown. "That's all well and good sir, but why?"

The inspector leaned back in the leather chair,
crossed his legs and absently tapped a pencil on
the desk blotter. "Try this out for size, sergeant.
It's my guess that, in January of 1942, when the
payments started, Marion Bundy did something
that was so out of character, she felt she had to
pay a blackmailer for nineteen and a half years to
prevent her father from finding out what she'd
done. And what's more, I'll bet you ten to one
the whole solution to these murders is tied up in
that one little act!"

"But sir, the only two left from that old group
are the colonel and Cecil Bundy, and from their

war records, both were fighting in other parts of the world in the winter of that year.''

"I know, Bucks, I know!" said the inspector. "But I don't intend to hit my head against a brick wall when there's an open gate staring me in the face. So let's go and see the colonel.''

A sharp rapping on the door temporarily abated their plans.

"Yes?''

Margaret stepped into the room. The look of annoyance on the inspector's face was not the greeting she had anticipated. "Am I interrupting anything?" she asked hesitantly.

Ronald Dobbs made no attempt to hide his irritation. "Miss Cathcart, why is it you have the uncanny ability to be at the wrong place at the wrong time?" he said none too kindly.

Margaret drew herself up to her full height. "My dear Inspector Dobbs," she said, "if anyone is to blame for my standing here at this particular moment, is it you! For two days I've been trying to see you, and each time I've come by, Sergeant Buckingham told me you weren't here. Personally, I'd just as soon not tell you my theory and let you figure out how it was done all on your own.'' Her head high, Margaret turned her heel and marched for the door.

The inspector threw up his hands in surrender. "Miss Cathcart, I apologize," he said contritely. "What with another murder on our hands, I'd forgotten all about your theory. You certainly chose a bad time, however. We're just on our way to see your cousin.''

"He left a minute ago," said Margaret.

Ronald Dobbs tried his best not to show his exasperation. If she hadn't come in when she did. . .! Well, the only thing to do was to make the most of the situation; he might as well hear her theory. But wait. She'd spent time here in the forties. Perhaps. . .?

"Miss Cathcart, you weren't by any chance in Kingscombe in the winter of 1942, were you?"

Margaret looked blank. "1942?" She shook her head. "I wasn't in Kingscombe at all during the war. Why do you ask? Has it to do with the murders?" she asked expectantly.

There she was meddling again! "Miss Cathcart," said the inspector patiently, steering her toward the door that Sergeant Buckingham obligingly held open. "I know I said I wanted to hear your ideas about who the murderer might be, but—"

"Murderer!" exclaimed Margaret. "I haven't even attempted to find out who it is!" She gave a superior sniff. "After all, that's *your* job." The inspector and sergeant exchanged glances. "*I* wanted to tell you that I know how someone got into Alicia's garden!"

Quickly, the sergeant closed the door. The inspector, still holding Margaret's arm, did an about-turn and led her to a chair. Seating her comfortably, he went around to his side of the desk.

"Now that's a solution I'd like to hear," he said. "In fact, if you can throw any light on this particular puzzle, I shall be eternally grateful." He poised his pen above the pad and waited. "Now?" he prompted.

Margaret, unaccustomed to this velvet treatment, looked from one man to the other and nervously cleared her throat. "Well, I've given this a lot of thought, and. . . well, I think it was a cat."

The inspector cocked an eyebrow. "You mean a cat-burglar-type cat?" he asked skeptically.

Margaret leaned forward enthusiastically, warming to her subject. "No. I mean an ordinary tom that probably has a long list of questionable ancestors." The inspector still looked doubtful but, undaunted, Margaret hastened on with her story. "Sometimes, Inspector, being a venturesome child has it advantages. I was that kind of girl, though I don't think you were that kind of boy—at least, you've changed a lot if you were," she said impishly.

"Miss Cathcart! We are not here to discuss my childhood! Get to the point," boomed Ronald Dobbs.

"I'm coming to it, I'm coming to it," said Margaret unhurriedly, "if you'll just be patient and listen. When I was a child, just about every household had a cat, and we children took great delight in teaching our pets little tricks. Now there was a large house near us, with a wall around it and a high wooden gate. We'd always heard grown-ups talk about how beautiful the garden was on the other side of the wall. Each day we passed the place on the way to or from school, and I longed to see this garden. Eventually I did. I never told anyone how I managed it—not even Elizabeth. Had she known, she would have skinned me alive. I used my old tom to disengage the latch." The inspector raised an inquisitive eyebrow.

"It's really quite easy to get a cat to do this," she hurried on. "People often lock themselves out of their houses with no way to get in except through the back garden. Why, I recall a few years ago how old Mrs. Petty out by Dover Road—"

''Miss Cathcart, please!'' roared a by now
highly exasperated inspector. ''Get on with it.
How does a cat open a latch?''

''I'll tell you if you'll stop interrupting!''
Margaret snapped. She took a breath. ''You put
the cat over the other side by means of a tree or a
storage-shed roof, then entice it to open the gate
by dangling a tasty morsel on the other side, just
above the latch. When the cat leaps up for the
food, his paws inevitably depress the latch and
the gate is opened!'' finished Margaret triumphantly.

There was a moment's silence. Finally, the inspector spoke. ''I don't see how it can work,'' he
said. ''You're saying the food should be just
above the latch. Supposing it isn't? Supposing it's
to the side, or too low, or too high? I mean, you
can't see where you've dangled this food.''

Margaret gestured impatiently. ''You have to
have a large enough morsel on the end of the
string to be sure its descent will be stopped by
the latch as you slowly slide the string down.
That's all. I know it works. I've done it.''

''It's not that I don't believe you,'' said the inspector. ''It's simply that I find it hard to imagine
a cat—''

''Oh, but it does! They do!'' cried Margaret.
''Try it. There are plenty of cats around here! See
for yourself!''

''I intend to,'' said the inspector. ''Thank you
very much, Miss Cathcart, I, er, think you've
been most helpful. Sergeant?''

Sergeant Buckingham walked over and opened
the door. Margaret rose with all the dignity she
could muster and followed the sergeant. At the
door, however, she stopped and looked directly

at Sergeant Buckingham. Then she said ever so sweetly, "Just remember, sergeant, you're a witness to the fact that Inspector Dobbs said he'd be eternally grateful."

As he closed the door, the sergeant allowed the trace of a smile to play on his lips. Ronald Dobbs, he thought, has finally met his match! When he turned back to his superior, however, it was a sober-faced sergeant who asked, "Do you think it's possible, sir?"

"I don't know," said the inspector, "but tomorrow I intend to prove or disprove her theory."

Sergeant Buckingham opened his notebook and hunted for a passage written in it.

"What are you looking for, Bucks?"

"I remembered something Miss Purdy told us last Saturday night. Oh, here it is, sir." The sergeant began reading. " 'I met Alicia Rochmere and she told me about her flowers being ruined. She said she knew who did it, but wouldn't tell me.' "

"Let's go see Miss Purdy," said the inspector.

Miss Purdy became flustered when asked if she had any ideas whom Alicia was referring to. "Well...I...that is.... I'd hate to point a finger where it doesn't belong...but...."

"Yes, Miss Purdy?" encouraged the inspector.

"Well, I wouldn't put this sort of thing past him, but just the same...."

"Who?" said the inspector, closing his eyes patiently.

"Well...William Lemly, the boy who lives next door to Alicia's. I happen to know that he and Alicia had had a few, er, misunderstandings in the past."

That evening they took young Lemly and two of his pals in for questioning. Three braggadocios who were ready to shout their innocence from the rooftops. . . until it was proven that William Lemly's plimsoll fit the plaster cast perfectly and that his cat had been trained to do just what Margaret Cathcart said a cat could be trained to do. They then became three subdued boys—not beaten by a long shot, however—who gave their misguided reasons for destroying people's property.

Their destruction was initially done for no other motive than spite. Not only did they confess to destroying Alicia Rochmere's garden, but also the plants in Marion Bundy's greenhouse. They'd derived a perverse pleasure from the fact that, subsequently, both these women became murder victims. Then, of course, they'd been most amused as they'd watched the inspector and the sergeant walk around and around Alicia's garden wall. Thus the temptation to move on to yet another victim was irresistible, and Mrs. Thompson of Priory Road was next.

"And I suppose you hoped she'd be murdered, too," snarled the inspector, before placing the boys in the hands of the local police.

When the inspector and Sergeant Buckingham returned to Harewood, Margaret met them with the news that the colonel had retired for the night. Sergeant Buckingham went on into the study as his superior stopped in the hall. For a moment, the inspector and Margaret looked each other squarely in the eye, each waiting for the other to speak—Margaret, with an "I told you so," and Ronald Dobbs, with a "you were right." Neither managed the feat, however, and it was

Margaret who finally turned away and, mumbling a good-night, headed for the stairs. The inspector turned and entered the study.

"I'll talk with the colonel first thing in the morning," he said, just as the telephone rang.

It was a call from the forensic laboratory. Almost a full drum of parathion had been recovered, but there was no way to figure out exactly how much had been drained.

A minute later, the inspector related the message to his sergeant, then sighed and said, "Well, if there's anyone else on the killer's list, it's likely that her, or his, dose is already waiting."

"It doesn't look good, sir," replied Buckingham. "How can we find it, even if it is prepared?"

The inspector poured himself a steaming cup of tea. "Well, I can assure you we aren't going to waste precious time running hither and thither." He poured milk into his tea and took a tentative sip. "No, Bucks, our only solution, as far as I can see, is to find the motive behind these killings and then, hopefully, make a quick arrest. In the meantime, we'll put a guard on the colonel."

"The colonel, sir?"

"Of course. Logically, he's next on the list. Other than Cecil Bundy, he's the only one left of the old group."

10

"ELIZABETH," SAID MARGARET, "were you at Harewood in the winter of 1942?"

It was mid-morning, and Elizabeth had retired to her room to catch up on some correspondence. Margaret was critically viewing herself left and right before the pier glass.

"1942?" echoed Elizabeth absently, looking up from her postcard-writing to glance at her sister. "You're really asking me to cudgel my brains. Why do you want to know?"

"Oh, something Inspector Dobbs said last night," Margaret said nonchalantly. "You know I think I'll put a rinse on my hair," she added, closely inspecting a few strands.

"I think that would be an excellent idea," said Elizabeth offhandedly, her mind once again preoccupied with her postcards.

"Hmm. It never hurts to help nature along a little bit. Not when you reach your forties," said Margaret, holding in her stomach muscles and eyeing her profile. "And I think I should buy a few new dresses; everything I own looks so dowdy."

Elizabeth put down her pen, and for the first time since the conversation began, really observed her younger sister. "You mean it, don't you?" she asked unbelievingly.

Embarrassed by her sister's show of incredulity, Margaret quickly walked over to the chair and plunked down in her usual graceless manner. "Of course I mean it!" she exclaimed. "You've been after me all these years to take more pains with my appearance, and when I finally agree to do so, you don't believe me!"

"It's not that I don't believe you're sincere, dear," said her sister quietly. "It's simply that I wonder what brought on this about-face."

"Nothing," said Margaret firmly. "I'm simply tired of the old me and would like a new image." She sat up straighter. "Anyway, that's not what I want to discuss. You didn't answer my first question. Were you here in the winter of 1942?"

While Margaret fidgeted, Elizabeth took several minutes sorting out her thoughts. Finally she shook her head. "No, I'm sure I wasn't. Charles wasn't here, anyway. Right after the New Year he was shipped to Africa."

"Damn!"

"Margaret!"

"I wanted to be able to impress the inspector and tell him what might have happened in the winter of that year," she said.

"Well, I'm afraid I can't help you," said Elizabeth, resuming her writing. "Until 1944, the last time I was here was Christmas, 1941. You'd been evacuated to the Midlands."

"And you didn't see or hear anything out of the ordinary?" asked Margaret.

"When?" asked Elizabeth.

"Christmas, 1941!"

Once more, Elizabeth looked up from her writing. "Not a thing. It was a very happy Christmas. Charles announced his engagement, too."

"Charles!" exclaimed Margaret. "I never even knew he was engaged!"

"You were away at school, my dear, and by the time things had settled down, it was all over anyway."

"But you could have at least told me!"

"Unfortunately, it lasted only a short time," said Elizabeth. Margaret opened her mouth, but her sister intercepted. "And before you ask me, no, I don't know why it was broken."

"Good heavens," said Margaret intrigued by this bit of family news. "Imagine! Charles! Engaged! Who was she?"

Elizabeth frowned. "I can't remember her name, Margaret, not after all these years. I never really knew her. Charles surprised us all—or perhaps just me. With the war and all, we'd been out of contact for a while, and after that Christmas, I never saw her again." She licked a stamp and stuck it firmly on a postcard.

"Try! Try to think of her name!" insisted Margaret. "It could be important!"

"Oh, for heaven's sake, Margaret!"

"Please, please Elizabeth, just think! No! No, wait I have a better idea! Be right back!" She hurried out of the room and minutes later was back with a photograph album under her arm. She pulled a chair next to Elizabeth's and opened the album. "I thought if we found a picture in here, it might jog your memory." She began to turn the pages. "Do you remember what she looked like?"

"As I recall, she was a pretty little thing, but I'm not sure I'd remember her," said Elizabeth, perusing each picture. "It was so long ago. . . . I can't see why it's so important now."

"I'm not sure it is, but we'll look anyhow," said Margaret.

They had thumbed through almost the entire album, and finally Elizabeth said, "It's no use. There isn't a picture of her."

"There are a few more pages yet," said Margaret, undaunted.

It was on the second-to-last page that they came across the newspaper clipping, tucked between the pages. It was an obituary. Margaret picked it up and began to read aloud.

"Eunice Freeman . . ." she said.

"That's it! That was the name of Charles's fiancée!" cried Elizabeth.

Margaret looked up. "She died last year," she said, "in a place called Waltham Dale." She glanced down at the card again, a frown of concentration forming on her brow. "Eunice Freeman . . . where have I heard that name recently?"

Her sister looked surprised. "Certainly not from Charles or myself. The subject of his fiancée is verboten as far as our cousin's concerned."

"No . . ." said Margaret. "It was someone else who was talking about it. Wait a minute . . . I'll remember . . . Mrs. Dawson!" she cried triumphantly. "She's the one! In the coach house the other day, Elizabeth, Mrs. Dawson said something about Eunice Freeman who got herself pregnant and moved away."

Elizabeth, following her sister's thoughts, looked aghast. "Margaret! You're not saying that Charles . . . !"

"Oh, hang it all, Elizabeth," said Margaret excitedly. "I'm not saying anything for certain. But let's face it, she was engaged to our cousin and it's not unlikely that he'd be the father!"

"That I won't believe!" said Elizabeth emphatically, putting pen and postcards aside. "Not that he couldn't be the father; but that he'd not face his responsibilities. It's absolutely ridiculous."

"Oh, darn it, I agree," said Margaret, slumping as though the wind had been knocked out of her. "Particularly since they were going to be married anyway." Then, trumphantly, "I have it! Someone else must have fathered the baby!" She jumped up and resumed her well-worn path. "And I suspect that if anyone had an inkling, it would be Ruth Dawson. There isn't much that escapes that woman." She picked up her raincoat from the chair. "I think I'll go have a little chat with her."

Elizabeth was, by now, fully caught up in Margaret's train of thought. "You know, Margaret, you're no doubt right about Mrs. Dawson, but I think you'll be sadly disappointed when you talk with her. You've forgotten she was a child in 1942."

Deflated once again, Margaret sank into the nearest chair. For a few minutes the two sisters sat in silence, each trying to solve the problem they'd created. Margaret was the first to speak. "I don't care if she *was* a child," she said, standing up and shrugging into her coat. "It's obvious that the situation was discussed in her presence, or she wouldn't know as much as she told me. I'm going over there to see her now. It certainly won't hurt."

"Oh, while you're out, would you mind posting these cards for me?" said Elizabeth, picking up her correspondence and handing it to her sister. "You know, Margaret, it's almost impossible to believe that Joyce Twickham won't be behind the counter anymore."

"I know," agreed Margaret. "Her cousin is taking over until things can be settled—the one who doesn't like the country."

Elizabeth grimaced. "I don't think she'll last long."

"Well, wish me luck," said Margaret at the door.

"Oh, I do," said Elizabeth. "And Margaret...."

"Yes?"

"Let's hope Mrs. Dawson's mother took as active an interest in people as her daughter does!"

"Amen!" said Margaret as she closed the door.

She found Mrs. Dawson in the coach house and she was more than willing to talk. The only trouble was, she really didn't know much about Eunice Freeman. As a child, Ruth had simply gleaned the fact that Eunice had left the village in disgrace, and her family had gone a short time later.

It was a disappointing interview, to say the least, and on her way to town, Margaret mulled over the past hour.

"Miss Cathcart!" Emily hurried across the road. Even the horror of discovering Miss Twickham the previous day couldn't dispel her spirits. "Oh, Miss Cathcart, I'm so glad to see you! Come in and have a cup of tea with me," she bubbled, guiding Margaret toward the tea shop. "With all that's been happening, I haven't even thanked you for letting me cry on your shoulder the other day...and did you know I'm engaged? John asked me to marry him! By telephone, no less! Of course, I've a hundred things to do before the

wedding! I'm going to London tomorrow.... Is
this table all right?''

Margaret, who'd acquiesced to being led along
by Emily, nodded her approval. This time it was
she who needed cheering up, and she couldn't
think of anyone at the moment she'd rather be
with than Emily. Her carefree happiness was
contagious. Over strong tea and cakes, they discussed Emily's wedding plans and future. All in
all, it had turned into a delightful afternoon.

"Goodness! Look at the time!" said Margaret,
picking up her handbag and postcards from the
table. "I have to be getting home. Elizabeth will
be wondering what's become of me."

For a moment Margaret shuffled the postcards
absently, scanning the pictures. "Now where on
earth did Elizabeth scare up this one? She said
she bought them all at Miss Twickham's."

"Let's see," said Emily, coming around to look
over the other woman's shoulder. The scene was
of a tree-filled valley, a tiny village nestled in its
bosom. Along the bottom, the letters almost
obliterated by the greenness of the foliage, was
printed, "Waltham Dale, Co. Durham."

"Miss Twickham had several postcards of
places up north," said Emily. "I asked her about
it one time and she said they were scenes of
places she knew as a child." Emily looked at the
card again. "Waltham Dale. That's where she
went last weekend," she mused, "to attend a
friend's wedding."

Emily was not prepared for the impact caused
by her statement. First, her companion looked
through her as though she no longer existed.
Then, Margaret's bright eyes focused on Emily.
Rummaging in her purse, she found a pound note

and put it on the table. "Emily, dear, I must run. There's money for the bill. I don't usually make a habit of this, you know...running out, that is...but somehow...the things I hear in this shop!" She shook her head in disbelief. "They astound me! Absolutely astound me!"

"Miss Cathcart..." began Emily.

"...and I think I'm on the way to catching a murderer! With your help, of course," she added graciously.

Emily, a question forming on her lips, was hushed by Margaret. "Wait until I've checked out a few things. You'll hear soon enough!" She gathered up the postcards and popped them into her bag. "It's been marvelous talking with you, and I wish you and John all the happiness in the world." She left Emily gaping, as she flew out the door.

She made it home in record time. Bursting into the Hall, she found Elizabeth in the morning room, relaxing with a novel. She put the book down when she saw Margaret.

"Did you get what we wanted?" she asked eagerly. "What did Mrs. Dawson have to say?"

"*She* had nothing to say. But I think I see a light. Where's Charles?"

"Why...he's with the inspector," said Elizabeth. Then, seeing Margaret was about to leave, she hastily added, "but I wouldn't disturb them if I were you."

"Well, I'm going to disturb them, Elizabeth, whether they like it or not, and Charles is going to tell me about Eunice Freeman!" She ran out of the room and down the stairs, leaving an astonished Elizabeth behind. Without knocking, she opened the study door and went in.

"Charles, have you told the inspector about Eunice Freeman, and did you know she and Miss Twickham lived in the same town?" she said.

"Miss Cathcart! You again!" thundered the inspector.

"Yes, me!" said Margaret, head high and feet planted firmly on the rug. "And I'm getting tired of helping solve your cases for you. This is absolutely the last one! You see, I've found a connection."

"Only a connection?" said the inspector softly.

His reaction surprised her. Why had his roar suddenly changed to a mew? "Well . . ." she began, suddenly not so certain of her stand. "It's a start, anyhow. And you see, you couldn't possibly know what I know," she said, her confidence returning.

"Oh, I don't doubt that, Miss Cathcart," said the inspector smoothly. He indicated a chair. "Here, do please sit down. But you see, the difference is, I already know who our murderer is! Now perhaps we can compare notes and see where we stand."

The colonel cleared his throat. "Harumph um . . . shall I continue?" He'd been most obliging. The inspector and his sergeant had already questioned him about the night of the recent party and he'd told them every detail he could think of but now he found himself telling them about another party many years ago.

After listening patiently, the inspector made two telephone calls: one to Waltham Dale; the other to Somerset House in London, the national registry office. When he hung up the phone, he was ecstatic. "We've got him cold!"

Relief in the room was evident.

"I need a cigar," said the colonel, taking an already opened box from the cupboard.

The inspector was out of his chair in two seconds flat. "Don't!" he shouted, grabbing the box from the colonel's hands. "When did you get these?"

"Well...." The colonel hesitated, slightly miffed by the inspector's rough handling. "I order several boxes at a time from London."

"Well, you're going to have to give them all to us," said the inspector, gathering up the others. "You'll have to buy new ones."

"But why?" sputtered the colonel.

"Because our murderer was very careful to poison only the things he knew his victim used personally," explained the inspector. "He had no intention of killing innocent people. These cigars, Colonel Hawkins, are your very personal items. You have them especially made for you, and I've noticed that you never offer them to anyone."

The colonel reddened. "I keep another brand on hand for visitors."

"Exactly, colonel, and I'm sure the killer knew that. He is a most thorough person."

They found parathion in one of the cigars in the opened box.

THE MURDERER DIDN'T OFFER any resistance, so his arrest was done with a minimum of fuss. They read him his rights and took him to the station, where he talked. As far as he was concerned, he'd accomplished his mission, and all was right with the world.

LATER THAT EVENING, the inspector addressed an attentive group assembled in the study.

"It all began at a Christmas party in 1941, when three people shattered a young girl's dreams: Charles Hawkins, because of mistrust and jeal-

ousy, and Alicia Rochmere and Marion Bundy,
because they didn't come to her aid when she
need them. This young girl was Eunice Freeman,
Charles Hawkins's fiancée, and her only crime
was helping her friend Marion Bundy, who was
in a jam. Marion had made an assignation with a
handsome young American soldier the colonel
had brought home several times before, this time
for the holidays. He was probably the only man
who ever won Marion Bundy's heart, and perhaps for this reason, she was blind to the fact
that he was a ladies' man and held no deep feeling for her; she, however, never forgot him!
Unfortunately for everyone, Marion's husband
obtained a last-minute leave and arrived shortly
before the planned meeting; in fact, the young
soldier had already excused himself and gone to
his room to await his ladylove. There was
Marion, her soldier boy waiting impatiently and
her soldier husband just arrived at the party.
Now, there were only two people who knew
about Marion's little fling: her best friends,
Eunice Freeman and Alicia Rochmere.

"So she asked Eunice to do her a favor: take a
message to the American soldier, explaining why
she was keeping him waiting. Eunice complied,
but her innocence and care to leave the door ajar
was her undoing. Missing his fiancée, the colonel
went looking for her."

The inspector glanced at Charles. "Colonel
Hawkins admitted today that he has a jealous
nature and a violent temper, which he has, fortunately, learned to control. But when he was a
young man and this volatile combination flared,
it sometimes had disastrous results, which is
what happened in this case. Another thing you

should keep in mind is that the accepted moral standards then were much different from today's.''

The inspector paused, took a breath and continued, "Anyway, hearing voices coming from the bedroom, the colonel pushed the door wider and saw his fiancée and his army buddy sitting together on the bed...and instantly jumped to the wrong conclusion. In a blind rage, he denounced her and broke the engagement. No one downstairs suspected a thing. When the colonel rejoined the party, he told them Eunice didn't feel well and his friend had retired for the night. In actual fact, Eunice had returned home, and the young soldier was hastily packing his bag.

"Colonel Hawkins, who had been on embarkation leave, left the next day, and by the time he'd regretted what he'd done and swallowed his pride, he was many miles away, in North Africa. He wrote Eunice to ask forgiveness, but the letter was returned address unknown." Once more the inspector paused. "Well, so much for the colonel's story; now we'll pick up the murderer's.

"The day after the episode, Eunice, hurt and angry, went to the two people she knew could straighten things out—Marion Bundy and Alicia Rochmere. Unfortunately for Eunice, and eventually for herself, Marion refused to tell Charles Hawkins the truth. As far as she was concerned, the girl was well rid of him. If he didn't trust Eunice now, he never would. Therefore, Marion couldn't see why she should put her own reputation in jeopardy by confirming Eunice's story.

"Now we come to Alicia Rochmere, the vicar's daughter. A sweet, timid little thing, who wouldn't hurt a fly. She knew Marion had planned the assignation, and it was also she who gave Eunice the present of Angelique, the music box that eventually meant Alicia's death. What happened to Alicia that day? Did she finally see a way out of her humdrum life? Did she perhaps long for luxuries she could see others had? Whatever the cause, she decided to grab for the golden ring...and wasn't stupid. She knew Marion's real reason for not telling the truth was not because of her husband's wrath, but because of her father's wrath. He'd cut her off without a penny if he knew what she had planned that night. So Alicia kept quiet, and for nineteen and a half years, from January, 1942, until July, 1961, when her father died, Marion Bundy paid Alicia Rochmere one hundred pounds a month to keep her silence.

"Miss Cathcart pointed out the fact that, when Eunice left Kingscombe, an angry young girl, the gossip mongers had a field day saying her departure was because she was pregnant. How these rumors get started, I don't know, but even then, her friends didn't come to her rescue and squelch the lies.

"Eunice married during the war, but like so many hasty marriages at that time, when the bombs stopped dropping and life settled down again, the two people involved found out they couldn't stand each other and got a divorce. This was fine for Eunice's husband, but by that time, she had a child to raise. She was living in Newcastle by then, and she took back her maiden name. For the next twenty-two years she worked hard, devoting her life to her offspring. Thirteen years ago, when her child had grown and left the nest, she took her meager savings and invested them in a small house in Waltham Dale. She died there last year, an embittered woman, leaving behind the one person who loved her—and who vowed to avenge the wrong that had been done.

"The murderer took his time planning, and he was certainly ingenious." The inspector stopped, assembling his thoughts. "I don't know if any of you have heard of parathion, but it's a highly toxic poison used in insecticides, and most elusive to detect. If poison were not suspected the cause of death could be written off as pulmonary edema.

"Now, how our murderer got hold of it is quite a story in itself. He witnessed a robbery attempt. Driving from Edinburgh to London one night, he'd parked his car by the curb for some sleep when he saw two men break into a truck whose driver was in a café. They'd unloaded one drum, when for some reason they suddenly left it by the side of the road and took off. Curious, our man went over to see what had frightened them. One look at the label told him. POISON. He'd found his weapon.

"The label also told him what sort of poison it was, and he went on to study its effects . . . and study his victims. Alicia Rochmere, even though a blackmailer—who never had the nerve to spend any of the money—was a sentimental little lady. Marion Bundy was vain, and Colonel Hawkins kept his own brand of cigars for himself. So the murderer prepared his packages. He didn't worry even when we knew about the poison. He felt secure in the knowledge that we couldn't connect him with the murders, and we probably never would have—except for Miss Twickham.

"Saturday night, after the colonel's party, she saw something that puzzled her, and being Joyce Twickham, she decided to get to the bottom of it. You see, she had been acquainted with Eunice Freeman in Waltham Dale. I say 'acquainted' because they weren't truly friends. Miss Twickham lived in the village only eleven months after Eunice moved there, but she did know Eunice had a son. She'd never met him, though, because that one year of their joint residency in Waltham Dale, he was working his way through the countries of Europe; when he did come back to England, he lived in London, but by that time, Joyce Twickham had already moved to Kingscombe, and her infrequent visits back north never coincided with his visits to his mother. Consequently, Eunice Freeman's son never associated Joyce Twickham with Waltham Dale until Saturday night. Imagine the mental anguish he must have experienced for three days, fearing the postmistress might connect him with the murders! That's why he went to the shop early Wednesday morning, and that's when Joyce Twickham should have kept her mouth closed. But instead, in her guileless way, she blurted out what she had seen on Saturday night and how she'd realized he was the son of her departed friend in Waltham Dale. No doubt, she was waiting for a pat on the back for her astuteness. Instead, she was stabbed with a hatpin."

"How awful!" exclaimed Emily.

The inspector nodded in agreement. "Especially when I doubt if she even connected him with the murders. But our murderer couldn't leave the one and only person alive in Kingscombe who knew his real identity. So he killed her."

"What was it she saw?" asked an exasperated Margaret.

"When Joyce Twickham was driven to the train station Saturday night, she'd raced 'round to the back of the colonel's car to help take out the luggage, and there was the damning evidence staring her in the face. You see, our murderer had packed the rubber suit, hoses, everything he'd used while handling the poison, into an old valise, which he put into the truck of the car. Imagine his anguish when he realized that Joyce Twickham had probably seen his real name, with Waltham Dale—the very place she was going to— boldly printed on the identity card in the celluloid pocket of the valise."

"His real name?" exclaimed Emily.

"Yes," said the inspector. "Frank Freeman. Not Frank Franks. The colonel's chauffeur."

HIS FIRST FREE DAY found the inspector driving to Harewood Hall. The lovely bright weather, however, was totally lost on Ronald Dobbs as he fought with his conscience at every twist and turn in the road. Why was he going to Kingscombe, he asked himself. Instinctively trying to rationalize his motives, he decided that his reason for driving all this way was to see the colonel and thank him for his hospitality...but personal feelings kept rippling the smooth surface of rationalization. Although he wasn't ready to admit it, even to himself, he knew it was Margaret Cathcart who was drawing him back.

Even after turning into the entrance lane of the Hall, he had thoughts of retreat, but then, suddenly, there was the portico and a somehow more attractive, younger-looking Margaret standing on the steps.

They spent a pleasant afternoon walking and chatting—he warned her not to bring up recent events and, surprisingly, she didn't. And now, after tea, he found himself complacently smoking his pipe as he leaned against the low stone wall of the patio, contentedly observing this remarkable woman. She looked about to burst with curiosity, and finally, she could contain herself no longer.

"What happened to Marion's soldier? Have you found him?" she asked.

"Oh, yes," replied the inspector. "We traced him to a cemetery in Arizona. He died of a heart attack six years ago."

Margaret's eyes saddened.

"You know, Miss Cathcart," said the inspector quietly, "everything pointed to the past, and it took me too long to realize it. The figurine Alicia Rochmere had given Eunice, and the scent of Ashes of Roses—the perfume that Franks, or Freeman, put in the poison he prepared for Marion Bundy. He finally told me his mother always associated the scent with the fateful night in Kingscombe, because the colonel had given her a vial of it that evening, and Marion had also received one from her soldier. That's probably why Mrs. Bundy was so ecstatic Saturday night; she expected to meet her old love, thinking he'd sent the lotion and the message." The inspector's eyes narrowed in retrospective contemplation. "Odd, isn't it, how one thing can mean so many different things to different people. For Eunice Freeman, Ashes of Roses held the stigma of bitterness and hatred. For Marion

Bundy, it brought back the joy of youth and love. Even the colonel associated it with times long ago. I've wondered since if, on that night Marion died, I'd followed up on his remark about Ashes of Roses bringing back memories, I would have been able to save Joyce Twickham.''

Margaret reached out and lightly touched Ronald Dobbs's arm. ''Don't dwell on something that can't be changed,'' she said quietly. ''You did your best.''

For a long moment their eyes locked, both of them feeling a closeness they'd never experienced. Finally, the inspector pushed himself away from the wall. ''I have to be getting back. There are a million and one reports to fill out.'' He reached out and took Margaret's hand. ''Miss Cathcart, looking back on it . . . .''

Margaret smiled and gazed up at him. ''Call me Margaret. Oh, and you'll be hearing from me,'' she said sweetly. ''After all, you're 'eternally grateful,' remember?''

Ronald Dobbs just smiled.

Be a detective.
See if you can solve the...

*R*aven House MINUTE MYSTERY

On the following page is Raven House
MINUTE MYSTERY #1, "A Lie Gets the Ax."

Every month each Raven House book will feature a
MINUTE MYSTERY, a unique little puzzler designed
to let *you* do the sleuthing!

Check your answer by calling (in U.S.A. only)
1-800-528-1404 during the months of August,
September and October 1981. Canadian and U.S.
residents may obtain the solution by writing any time
during or after this period to:

Raven House MINUTE MYSTERY
1440 South Priest Drive
Tempe, AZ 84281
U.S.A.

A LIE GETS THE AX

"The body's under the woodpile, but remember—you gotta keep me outa this," whined Stig Carona, casting shifty eyes at Professor Fordney and Inspector Kelley. Sniffing through a nose that an ungenerous nature had placed at an unlovely angle and licking lips cut on the bias, Stig twisted his greasy cap in nervous fingers.

An hour later the three men got out of a police car and walked to a clump of bushes in Wilson's woods.

"Bill and Jake were fightin' in front of that shack over there," Stig explained, pointing to a clearing. "Jake knocked Bill down, then grabbed an ax. When Bill got up Jake hit him over the head with it a couple of times. Then he dragged the body toward the shack. He must've thought he heard somethin' 'cause he propped it up against the house and walked over this way. I knew if he found me here I'd get what Bill got, so I lammed to the road, jumped in my car and went for the cops."

Fordney observed bloodstains on the shack about three feet from the ground, which appeared to bear out Stig's story. Some freshly cut firewood spattered with dark stains lay near a chopping block.

Opening the door of the shack the professor was about to enter when Kelley called from the yard. "The body's under the woodpile, all right. Gad, what a sight!"

But Fordney's interest at the moment was not the body but a bright, clean, shining ax standing in the far corner of the shack's single room. Carrying it by its battered handle, he took it outside. At the professor's quiet words Stig turned with a startled look.

"Unless," said Fordney, "you want to be placed under arrest for murder immediately, you will tell us the truth about this crime."

How did Fordney know Stig's account was untrue?

From **Minute Mysteries** by Austin Ripley
Copyright © 1949 by Opera Mundi. Paris

Move to

Raven House...

...Home of the Finest in Mystery Reading!

Millions of fans can't be wrong...

For more than a century and a half,
tales of mystery and detection
have captured the imaginations
of readers the world over.

Now Raven House Mysteries

...offers the finest examples
of this entertaining popular fiction —
in a brand-new series that contains
everything from puzzling whodunits
to stories of chilling suspense!

Reviewers across the country rave about Raven House!

"...impressive writing..."
—*Ellery Queen Magazine*

"...a joy to suspense buffs."
—*West Coast Review of Books*

"...fiendishly clever..."
—*Quality*

"...well worth the [price]..."
—*Jessyca Russell Gaver's Newsletter*

"...the best news in years for the paperback mystery field."
—*Wilson Library Bulletin*